Taken in Hand

Shannon West

and

LL Brooks

DEDICATION

To the J's

Acknowledgments   D.w. Skinner, Cover Photographer

1

"You've got to be kidding me. No fucking way!"

"Sit down, Corporal Williams, and stop being so dramatic. Are you homophobic?"

"No, not at all." The handsome young detective ran a hand through his short, russet brown hair and took a seat in front of his chief's desk. "I'm not prejudiced and to each his own. Hell, I support everyone's rights. But living in the same house with another man and pretending to be his submissive lover? Are you kidding me?"

"You know this sick son of a bitch we're after has killed another professor and his partner, and that makes a total of four men. Four men in my town in the past two months. It's intolerable. We haven't declared it, as yet, but I'm sure we've got a fucking serial killer on our hands. Yesterday we got one hell of a lead. We found out another professor received a threat in the mail just before the first killing, and he's telling us the latest victims did as well. If the letters connect to the killings, we have a chance to not only save his life, but catch the killer."

"What kind of threat? How come we're hearing about it from this other professor?"

"The most recent victims and the English professor were friends, and we found out about the notes when we interviewed him after the murders. No sign of the victims' note, but the professor showed us his copy--a piece of paper with verses from a Bible cut and pasted to the page, along with a warning at the bottom of the page to 'give up your sinful ways or the wrath of the redeemer will force your salvation,' or some shit, also cut and pasted. Phillips has the originals. Before you ask, no fingerprints are on the page other than the professor's. It has an Atlanta postmark, and the warning was clipped from an Atlanta paper. The Bible verse came from a cheap version, available in several of the big retail chain stores. No leads in any of it, yet,

1

though forensics is still working on it. We're working on establishing whether or not the first couple received a letter."

"I see."

"What I want to try is an undercover operation. Someone in the house with the professor, posing as his lover. I think you'd be perfect. Your presence there could draw out the killer or get him to make a move. If the professor agrees to what I have in mind, we can't afford to let the opportunity slip out of our hands."

Chad shifted positions in his chair uncomfortably. "What do you mean, I'd be perfect?"

"C'mon Williams, you're young, nice looking—believable. We're thinking seeing the professor take a new lover will set the killer off again, especially in light of the warning."

"Okay, fine, I understand, sir, but why me? Why not Phillips or Johansen? They've been in on this case from the beginning."

The chief leaned back in his chair to survey him. "Phillips is pushing sixty years old. Johansen is almost fifty and not exactly in the best physical shape of his life, as he'd tell you himself. This professor is young, nice looking, and no one would believe Phillips or Johansen could possibly be his preferred partner."

Settling back in his chair, Chad was unable to argue with the logic. Phillips was getting older, as was Johansen, who'd also put on quite a bit of weight in recent months. Neither of them exactly fit the description of the previous victims, all of whom had been men in their twenties and thirties. Also the victims up to this point had been gym-toned and nice looking. And they were all gay. Gay men in D/s relationships. Damn it, what the hell was kicking his pulse up?

Chad had fought against the idea he might be more than a little bi-curious since his college days. Too damn scared and freaked out to experiment, he had pushed the idea he was attracted to men more than women way down deep inside himself. So deep he rarely thought about it anymore. Okay, so he cruised an occasional porn site on the internet. Lots of guys looked at porn. It didn't mean a thing. Gay porn? The evil little part of him kept popping up with an inner dialogue, pestering him again. Porn that involved two men, one wearing leather, with the other tied down and helpless?

"Okay!" Chad said too loudly, to drown out the voice in his head. The chief stared at him in alarm. Quickly clearing his throat, Chad continued. "I mean, uh…okay, I'll at least meet with the guy and see if it's plausible."

The chief opened a file on his desk. "His name is Adam Morrison. He's a professor of…" He looked down to check his notes. "Renaissance Literature at the University. One of the victims was not only a colleague but also a close personal friend, which is why he knew about the threat. With this threat to him and the subsequent murder, he's calm enough, but a little concerned and rightfully so. He volunteered to do whatever he could to help us find the killer when we interviewed him yesterday. If we can convince him to pose as your partner in a relationship, we might be able to entice the killer to show himself. Of course, you can assure him he'll have round the clock surveillance, as well as security cameras outside, and you'd be on the inside to protect him at all times."

"This guy has definitely been cleared as a suspect?"

"Absolutely. Solid alibis for all the murders. He has a confirmed alibi for the first murder, and he was in front of a classroom full of students when the last one was committed. No, he's solid. Seems to be a nice enough guy too. I think you'll get along fine with him. I know you haven't been on the case and only have a general idea of what's been going on." He handed Chad a business card, along with the case file on the murders. "Look over the notes and reports to familiarize yourself with all the details. You won't be doing much investigation, but you still need to know what's going on to be able to recognize possible important details that might come up. That's the professor's numbers. Call him and set up a meeting today. If you think it will work after talking with him, we can get you moving on this thing right away."

Chad took the card and frowned down at it. It was a simple white business card with the man's name, his office and his cell numbers embossed on the front, along with the University of Georgia logo. Nothing there to make him feel a chill slip down his spine or cause the slight tremor in his hand. Why the fuck was he freaking out about this? He needed to get a grip and fast. The chief was giving him a questioning look, not the first in the last couple of weeks either. Chad had to admit he'd been working on a short fuse lately, losing his temper and being aggressive enough with one suspect he'd nearly ended up being on report. Though he didn't want to admit it, the stress of the job was getting to him, too many murders, too many people doing horrible things to each other.

He got to his feet, pocketed the card, and with a wave to the chief, made it out to his desk without embarrassing himself further. Pulling the card from his pocket, he stared down at it for a moment feeling his heart beating too fast. Damn it, what was the matter with him? He'd call the guy and set up a meeting. No problem. He checked his watch and saw that it was almost eleven o'clock. The guy would probably be in class now, so it would be a good time to call and just leave a message. Ask him to get in touch.

With that plan in mind, Chad dialed the number of his office at the University, expecting it to go to voice mail. Instead a warm, sexy voice answered. "Adam Morrison."

Thrown off guard, Chad hesitated a fraction too long. The voice spoke again, with irritation. "Hello?"

"Yeah, this is Detective Chad Williams with the Athens-Clarke County Police Department. My chief gave me your card."

"Oh, hello, Detective. Of course. What can I do for you?"

"The chief said you might be interested in helping us out with our investigation, especially in light of this threat you've received. Can we meet somewhere soon to discuss the possibility?"

There was only a brief hesitation before he agreed. "All right. I can meet you for lunch today. I can be there by one o'clock."

"Where?"

"The End Result on Clayton Street?"

"Yeah, of course. I'll be there at one, then."

The line went dead, and Chad found himself staring down at the receiver in his hand. Hell, he wasn't much for small talk himself, but at least the guy could have said goodbye. Good to know the professor wouldn't talk his head off. He hung up, opening the case file to study it.

Phillips or Johansen had done a good job of working up profiles on all of the victims. Two had been professors at the University, though in different departments, one in history and one in journalism. One of the partners was a graduate assistant, the youngest, and in his early twenties. Another was an attorney in town. None of the men had been older than thirty-eight.

Both couples had been in openly homosexual, committed relationships, and their bodies had been found close together on the floor, tightly bound with ropes in an intricate style known in Japanese shibari, associated with BDSM practices. Though they'd all been beaten, death came as the result of exsanguination, according to the coroner, from the cutting off of their genitalia.

With no sign of forced entry in the premises, the primary theory was the men had known their killer and perhaps invited him in. Burn marks on their bodies told them a stun gun had been used to incapacitate them, those marks nearly obliterated by the viciousness of the beatings. Though their pants had been stripped down to their knees, none of the men showed signs of rape. Time of death for all four was estimated to be between ten pm and four am.

The severity of the beatings and mutilations indicated a personal, out of control rage. All had been kept silent with a type of gag used in BDSM called a ball gag. The search was on for the manufacturer as a possible lead.

Both couples had ties to the University and they socialized together from time to time. One couple frequented a private sex club in Atlanta. He filed that bit of information away to be examined later. Despite the thorough job Phillips and Johansen had done of interviewing friends and family, University personnel—including those with limited contact such as delivery people—and students, even the club one pair belonged to, nothing presented a red flag. They'd had run into one dead end after another. It was time to try something a little bolder to draw the killer out, instead of waiting for the next victims to turn up.

Chad glanced down at his watch and cursed softly under his breath. He had been so absorbed in the reports he'd let the time get away from him. He had only fifteen minutes to get across town to the restaurant where he was meeting the professor. He pulled on his jacket and hurried out to his car, hoping the traffic wouldn't be too bad that time of day. It wasn't too far distance wise, but the restaurant was near the old campus and the downtown area, where traffic could get heavy at times.

Luck was with him. He not only made it to the area in ten minutes, but he had no trouble getting a parking spot on the street outside. What were the odds this close to lunchtime? Silently sending up thanks to whatever gods might be responsible for his good fortune, he went inside the warm interior and scanned the occupants for his man. Correction, for the professor, he reminded himself uneasily.

The restaurant, known for its excellent food, was pretty crowded, but he picked out a man right away he thought might be the one. He was maybe in his late thirties, balding a little on top, with glasses he wore on the bridge of his nose as he looked over the menu. Chad took a step toward him when the man was joined by two women, one of whom appeared to be his wife or girlfriend by the squeeze she gave to his hand.

A warm hand landed on his shoulder, and Chad turned to gaze up into a pair of deep brown eyes. The man was at least six-two, with a trim and toned body, a good four inches taller than Chad. He had artfully mussed brown hair, a full mouth, and movie-star good-looks. He wasn't smiling, however, and didn't look too happy to be there. Fine lines around his eyes showed he wasn't quite as young as Chad first judged him to be, and Chad adjusted his estimate to put the man in his mid-thirties.

"Sgt. Williams, I presume? I'm sorry if I kept you waiting. A student came to my office without an appointment." He frowned a little over the words, and Chad was glad he hadn't been the hapless student.

He extended his hand. "Nice to meet you, Professor. Thanks for taking the time to speak with me."

Morrison nodded curtly, accepting his hand and looking around for the hostess. "Let's find a seat, shall we, and we can talk." He looked down at his hand still encased in Chad's grip and narrowed his eyes a bit. Chad realized with a start he'd been holding on for far too long. He dropped the hand quickly and took a step backward, putting more distance between them.

A tiny smile played at the corners of the professor's mouth as he waved down the hostess and had a word with her. She led them to a booth in the back. Handing them their menus, she promised to send their waitress before bustling back to the reception area.

Morrison met his eyes over the top of the menu. "What are you going to have, Detective? The black bean soup here is excellent, as is the frittata."

"Just a hamburger," Chad said, folding his menu.

The professor pursed his lips a bit and frowned again, making Chad feel like he expected him to order what he suggested, though he didn't like black beans and had no fucking clue what a frittata even was. A hamburger obviously didn't meet with this guy's approval. And why did that bother him, damn it? He didn't need the guy's okay on anything.

Chad settled back in the booth and glanced around the restaurant. About three-quarters full, people talked and laughed quietly around the room. It had a nice vibe, with its old brick walls and snowy white tablecloths, upscale without being pretentious. Chad liked it right away. Even though the place had been in town for years, he'd never been there. He usually didn't hang out in downtown, preferring to grab something at a drive-through if he ate out after work. Since he'd split with his last girlfriend six months before, he hadn't gone out much at all.

The waitress appeared, and he ordered a sweet iced tea and a hamburger, while the professor ordered the frittata with water.

"I'm starving," he confided across the table, adding a charming little smile. "I had an early class after my workout this morning, and I didn't have time for breakfast."

Chad took in the broad shoulders and the hint of well-defined clavicle showing beneath his shirt. This guy worked out all right. "Yeah, you look like you exercise a lot," he commented and was instantly puzzled by why the hell he'd felt the need to comment. More than that, why did the professor make him uncomfortable? He reminded himself this was a work situation, and there was no need for him to feel bothered by a simple observation even if the guy was gay and likely to take his comment wrong. Police officers were taught to observe. No need for the urge to squirm as the professor gazed across the table at him. Get down to business, damn it.

"Thanks for meeting me, Professor Morrison."

"No problem. I told the other officers I spoke with that I was willing to help any way I could. Lt. Johansen and Philips, I believe. Where are they, by the way? Are they still on the case?"

"They're still primaries on the case, yes, but I've been assigned to work with you."

"With me?" One perfect eyebrow rose. "For what exactly? Consultation?"

"That and more—if you'll agree to it."

Chad leaned forward slightly to tell him the chief's idea only to straighten when the waitress arrived with their drinks and food. She put everything down and asked if there was anything else she could bring them, her attention centered on Chad. "Are you sure you have everything you need? I'll be glad to get you whatever."

Chad nodded, looking down at his plate. "No, looks fine, thanks." She finally left, throwing a flirtatious smile over her shoulder and twisting her hips a bit more than was probably necessary as she walked away. Disinterested in the show, Chad caught amused speculation in his companion's regard.

"You were saying, Detective?" the professor asked.

Irritation put an added crispness in his voice. "My chief had a little something different in mind other than consultation."

"Oh?"

"He's hoping you'd agree to a bit of an undercover operation. We're taking the threat you received very seriously."

"Good, because I am too," he said, his voice grim.

Chad nodded. "We need to draw the killer out, make him do something to give us some kind of trail to follow. Right now we're at a dead end."

"What do you have in mind?"

Chad took a deep breath and held the professor's gaze. Christ, he didn't want to do this. "You and me. We'd pretend to be…uh…boyfriends. See if we can draw the killer out."

Morrison put down his fork and stared across the table with a cold glint of steel in his eye. "Boyfriends? Seriously? Using me as the bait? Are you out of your mind?"

Chad blinked at him for a moment, feeling relieved. Still he had a job to do. "The chief thought you might. He said you would possibly…"

Morrison held up a hand. "I did say I was willing to do what I could, but this is …"

As much as Chad wanted to drop it right there, in good conscience, he couldn't. "Look, I understand your concerns, but we would mitigate the danger involved for you in this. You'd be under continuous surveillance, and I'd be there in the house with you."

"Excuse me, what do you mean by you'd be in my house?"

"He only seems to target couples living together. As I said, I'd be there whenever you are. We can almost guarantee your safety."

"Almost?"

Deciding to press for whatever slight advantage he could, he caught Morrison's gaze. "One of the men was a personal friend of yours. Isn't that right? And it seems the killer maybe bypassed you since you and your last boyfriend broke up. If you were to take another one, he might set his sights on you."

His lips tightened, and a dark glare swept over Chad. "I had a sub who lived with me for a time. I didn't have a boyfriend. And I'm not sure I'm willing to put myself at risk as a target."

7

Chad nodded and pressed his napkin to his lips. Fine, he'd made the pitch. "Okay. I understand. It was a lot to ask. I'll pay for all this and not take up any more of your time." He slid about halfway out of the booth before the man across from him touched his hand. "You give up pretty easily. Weren't you going to remind me how dangerous this monster is? Tell me about my civic duty or mention how these murders affect the entire LGBT community? Not to mention the reputation of the University itself? Try to pile on some worry and guilt?"

Chad might have thought the professor was playing with him, except for the haunted look in his eyes. He was worried and trying to hide it. "You said no. I'm not here to beg you or pressure you into it."

"Oh, for God's sake, Detective Williams, all right. I'll do it—for all of the above reasons, including the fact John Anderson was a good friend of mine. I knew him since we were undergrads together."

His eyes clouded, and Chad wondered if Morrison had ever been involved romantically with Anderson. Something had sure been going on behind those beautiful brown eyes when he said his name. Beautiful eyes? Shit, what the hell was wrong with him?

"Though I'm not sure how this will help," Morrison continued. "Surely you don't think any of my friends have anything to do with this."

Chad slid back over into the booth. "Someone sent those letters, someone who knows details about your personal life, just as they did your friends. You understand this means I'd have to move into your home temporarily?"

Morrison sighed. "Yes, I got that. I guess that will work, so long as you keep your presence as non-intrusive as possible. I value my privacy, and I wonder just how real this threat is to me personally. None of my friends would be capable of committing a crime like this."

"Four men are dead, Professor. I'd call that pretty real. With each of the murders, there was no sign of forced entry, indicating the victims knew their killer."

"Points taken, but no cameras or listening devices inside my home."

"I'll inform the chief of your preferences. In the meantime, if you could make me a list of anyone and everyone who knows about your lifestyle, so we can start checking them out."

"For God's sake, I don't have time for that. A lot of people know about it. I don't keep it a secret though I don't advertise my personal life at work."

"Maybe so, but what about the club one couple belonged to? Do you know anything about it?"

"I'm a member."

"Have you noticed anyone there paying particular attention to you lately?"

"No, but of course I've participated in activities there, where the whole idea is to get people to notice you."

"I see."

The professor laughed shortly. "I doubt it, but I suppose if you're to become my partner, you'll be getting a quick education in the lifestyle."

Chad felt the blush all the way to his toes. "If you're talking about the fact that you're gay, I have no problem with pretending I am."

Morrison leaned back in the booth and regarded him closely. "I wonder if you have any real idea of what you're getting yourself into. My partners in the past have all been required to live the lifestyle twenty-four-seven, both at home and in the club. All my close friends know this. There would be no question of hiding it or deviating from my usual habits."

"Hiding what?" Chad leaned across, lowering his voice instinctively in puzzlement. "What do you mean by the lifestyle? What exactly do you live twenty-four-seven?"

The professor smiled, looking just a bit like a large cat with canary feathers caught between its teeth. "The BDSM lifestyle. Aren't you familiar with it? I would have thought that since you're working this case, you'd know more about me."

Chad's insides tied in a knot. No, he didn't know about living that kinky all the time. That little piece of information hadn't been in the file. "I'm a Dom, and if you want to pretend to be my partner, that makes you the sub." The professor continued, leaning forward slightly, holding Chad's gaze, and not releasing it. "Bondage and Discipline, Domination and Submission, Sado-Masochism—that's what BDSM stands for, Detective. Have you heard of it?"

Morrison's lips were turned up in a little smile, no doubt to annoy Chad. At the same time a spicy, woodsy scent floated across the table, making Chad's crotch tighten unaccountably.

Morrison laughed out loud at Chad's expression. "What's the matter? Rethinking staying at my house and posing as my lover?"

"Very funny," Chad said, his voice tight and irritated. "Of course, I've heard the term."

Morrison raised one eyebrow and leaned back, his gaze almost predatory, giving Chad the feeling he was playing with him.

"As I said, all of my friends, anybody who would be invited to my home, knows of my interests. If you want to make people think this is a real relationship, you'd have to act the part."

Chad knew the man was enjoying his discomfiture. Maybe to shock him, maybe to wipe the smirk off his face, he glared at him and clipped out one word, "Fine."

The eyebrow rose again. "Fine? You realize that means whenever someone comes to my home or we go to the club, you might have to be naked except for your collar?" He gaze moved up and down, over what there was visible of Chad above the table. "I suppose we could get by with a jock strap for you."

A hot blush traveled up Chad's neck, and he almost choked over a sip of his tea. Even as he sputtered and tried to catch his breath under the amused gaze of the professor, he refused to back down from the son of a bitch. "You just won't invite people over while I'm there then, will you?"

"But Detective, wouldn't that just negate the entire idea? I mean, you'd be there to be seen, surely. It's a shame to hide a beautiful body like yours anyway."

Those damn brown eyes fucking glittered at him. How was it possible for someone so good looking to be such an ass? "Why don't you let me worry about that, Professor? I realize you're having a good time at my expense right now, but this isn't my idea of a laughing matter. People have died, and I want to help put a stop to it."

For the first time since he'd sat down at the table, Chad thought he scored a direct hit. Morrison's expression sobered instantly, and he nodded. "You're right, of course. Nothing about this is amusing, is it? It's tragic and horrible and disgusting. I apologize, Detective Williams."

"Let's back this up a little, okay? So you are agreeing to do this thing? To let me act as your partner? Move in with you?"

Morrison sighed. "Yes, I suppose, though as I said, I value my privacy, making this is a major concession for me. I also want the bastard caught. So, yes, I guess I'll do this thing."

Chad suffered some conflicting emotions. If Morrison had said no that would have been a way out his chief couldn't argue with. Still, as irritating as the guy was, it was Chad's job to see it through. "Okay." He huffed out a breath. "So I guess I have a few questions about all this to help me understand."

"Fire away, Detective." The glitter was definitely back in those eyes. He really did seem to be enjoying Chad's embarrassment.

"Okay, so this BDSM—it's a lifestyle for you."

"Yes, for the past few years. The lifestyle does appeal to me. As I said, I lived it with my last two subs."

"I understand you aren't involved right now, with a boyfriend or whatever." Chad had to admit to feeling almost relieved, though he didn't want to examine that too closely, telling himself it just made things simpler.

Morrison looked up at him and held his gaze just a fraction too long. "No, Detective, I'm not involved with anyone. And I wouldn't exactly call my subs boyfriends, either. It's a whole other dynamic for me. I had boyfriends when I was younger, but those relationships tend to get complicated. D/s relationships are simpler, in a way, though they tend to get serious fast. Sharing that much intimacy with another person is different from any other kind of relationship. I care for my subs, of course, but love…" He shrugged and fiddled with his napkin. Finally raising his head, he pinned Chad with a look. "Are you currently involved?"

Chad cleared his throat. "Look, if we're going to be working so closely together over the next few days or weeks, you should call me by my first name. It's Chad, and no, I'm not seeing anyone."

Taking a sip of water, Morrison gazed over the rim of the glass at him. "All right, Chad. You may call me Adam, though once we start this, it'll be better for you to get in the habit of calling me Sir." Another twinkle in his eyes, and Chad glared.

"You really do want to bust my chops over this, don't you?"

Adam laughed out loud, a surprisingly young, happy sound that had Chad fighting not to smile along with him. "I'm sorry, Chad, but you're so damn vanilla." He wiped a tear from his eye and glanced up at him. "I'm wondering if any of my friends will even believe you could possibly be my sub."

"You just tell me what to do, and I can do my job."

Adam leaned back and gave him the predatory look again. "Oh, I'm sure."

Chad chose to ignore that remark and took out a small notebook from his jacket pocket. "Mind if I take a few notes?"

Adam waved a languid hand at him.

"How deeply were your friends into this lifestyle? We have information that at least one of the couples belonged to a sex club in Atlanta called Dungeons."

"A BDSM club," Adam corrected gently. "John was, yes. He and Eddie, his partner, went to Dungeons frequently, though we never played together. Bradley Stevens and his partner, Tom, weren't members of the club, though from what I've heard, they practiced at least some kind of D/s behavior in their home. Tom was an attorney here in town. I saw them sometimes, but we weren't what I'd call close friends. I just knew them when I saw them."

Chad was writing furiously, but he paused and shook his head. "This club—Dungeons? Really?"

"I didn't name the club."

Shrugging at the curtness in his tone, Chad tried to concentrate on business. "What do you mean by you didn't play together?"

"Role play. That's what happens in the clubs. Doms take their subs to the clubs to watch scenes or to play out a scene themselves, or they find someone there to play with. Singles join in as well, but it's the couples who seem important in this instance. It's not unusual to have multiple partners or to play with each other's subs, though some are monogamous, of course." Reacting to the look on Chad's face, Adam sat forward. "I realize this is all new to you, but you have to realize this is totally consensual. Scenes are negotiated well in advance. Doms display their partners sometimes because they're proud of them. Some subs like to show off their submission. It's exhibitionist, yes, voyeuristic, but the sub and the Dom agree to this up front when they make out their contract."

"Contract?"

"Of course. It's in place to protect both parties. It spells out exactly what each of them expect and require from the relationship. They negotiate, write it all down, and both sign it."

"Okay, sorry. I'm having a hard time understanding what goes on in the…uh…sub's head. Why would anybody let someone hurt them?"

"Some subs like pain. There's a difference between being harmed and being hurt. Not all subs like pain, just as not all bondage and dominant relationships involve S & M. Bondage can refer to Japanese shibari, handcuffs, cages, and so forth."

Chad nodded. "Shibari? That kind of rope work was used on the victims."

"It's used frequently. Dominants like to control their subs. As for the sado-masochism part of the equation, not everyone is into that, though most do enjoy some mild S&M. Others don't like pain at all. Remember the domination and submission part of the BDSM acronym. For some couples, the control and submission is the key. Submissives like to make their partners happy, and it's not just in the bedroom. You hear people talk about caretaker personalities, and that's part of it, of course. Submissives find satisfaction in giving themselves to their Doms, but the Doms have to earn that kind of trust. The Dom doesn't have all the power, by any means. The sub chooses to whom they give their trust and devotion, and they can put a stop to all of it with one word. Subs have safe words they can use if the play gets too intense or more than they can handle. They allow it to happen on their terms, because as I said, it's all negotiated. Some people who aren't in committed relationships like the safety net of the club scene. If the play gets too intense, or the Dom is ignoring safe words, there are people around who will pull them out of the scene. Dungeon masters perform that function—like bouncers. They're there to ensure everything is safe and consensual."

He caught Chad's gaze and held it. His voice was low and incredibly intimate, even though people were talking and eating all around them. "Imagine giving yourself to someone like that. Allowing them to take their pleasure with you and take away all of your control, relieving you of the necessity to make even the simplest of decisions. In return, they give you more pleasure than you thought possible and give you the satisfaction of knowing you've been taken in hand, taken care of completely, with no worries except how to please your master and give him everything he wants, everything he needs, things only you can give him. In return for pleasing him, he takes you to peaks of pleasure you never even knew existed."

Mesmerized by what he was hearing, Chad leaned closer. A meaningful silence hung thick in the air between them when the professor finished. Chad could feel his heart beat faster, louder in his ears, thinking how welcome it would be sometimes to be able to let go and have someone else make all his decisions. What a relief it would be.

What the hell? He jerked up straight. What was he thinking? He snapped his notebook shut. "You've answered some of my questions for now. Uh, do you go to this Dungeons place very often?"

"I go usually once a week, on Saturday nights. As my sub, you would naturally accompany me. Will you be able to do that, Chad?"

He raised his chin and met the professor's eye straight on. "Sure, why not? As you said, it's role play, but let's get something straight, it will not be twenty-four-seven. In public I do my job, but when we go to your club, you will not take part in any trading or scenes. You will say whatever you have to for your friends to accept that. In private, I do not play any boy-toy role for your enjoyment."

"You don't set the terms or give me orders, and don't flatter yourself, Detective. Your body is nice, yes, but I don't think you're strong enough to be a sub. Not my sub, anyway, but understand, if we do this, you don't get to make the rules. My house, my rules, and you need to be trained properly before I display you at my club. I have my own reputation to consider. If you're not willing to put yourself under my control, this is not going to work."

Chad made an angry sound, and Adam held up a hand. "I have no desire for a—what was it you called it? A boy-toy? I like men."

They sat in silence for a long moment, staring at each other. Chad had a feeling a challenge had been laid down and he had no response to it.

Adam finally released his gaze and threw his napkin on the table. "I hate to run, but I do have a class this afternoon. If you have any other questions, you have my card."

"Yeah, sure. Thanks for coming, sir."

The second the word hit the air, he wanted to bite his tongue. To cover, he slid out along with the professor, though he'd barely touched his burger. He stood in front of the man and stuck out his hand. Adam looked down at him and smiled, taking the offered hand and holding it for a brief moment longer than necessary before dropping it.

"I'll wait for your call, Chad," he said and pointed to the gun and badge attached to Chad's belt. "Leave those at home."

* * * *

Adam Morrison stepped out of the restaurant into a cold breeze and shivered. His hand still tingled from touching Chad Williams, even so briefly. God, the man was delicious. From the first moment he'd seen him from the back standing in the entryway, he'd admired his body. He wasn't overly tall, only about five-ten, but he was trim and muscular, though not in a muscle bound way. Even without the badge and gun, he looked like a cop, with his black pants and plain shoes, topped by a leather jacket. His bronze colored hair was a little long for most cops he'd seen. Did that indicate a problem with authority? When he'd first turned around, Adam had to take a step back. He was gorgeous, with high cheekbones, perfect, full lips, and incredible blue eyes, the rare, pale, icy blue kind. His skin was light and translucent. It would blush up beautifully, showing every mark of his master's hand.

Oh yes, he was every inch a sub, whether he knew it or not. As a matter of fact, he wasn't sure Chad even knew he was gay. There had been a moment when they first shook hands that Chad had caught and held his gaze, not looking away until Adam challenged him by staring back at him directly. Almost immediately, he'd lowered his gaze. Classic sub behavior, though the man was completely unaware of it.

Adam was pretty much taken by everything about the young man, even the way he asked his questions. Brash and assertive, yet there was the fascination he'd shown when Adam explained the Dominant/submissive relationship. Just thinking about having him naked in his home made Adam's cock thicken in his jeans. He'd teased Chad, watching for the signs and finding them. Chad had a lot to learn, and Adam was tempted to be the one to teach him. Even though he had no desire to get into a relationship, he had a sudden image in his mind of Chad kneeling on a pillow at his feet, those big blue eyes gazing up at him trustingly, and Adam had to adjust himself. This investigation might be even more than Adam bargained for if his unexpected reaction to the young man was any indication. He had a feeling he'd be disappointed if he ignored his attraction.

2

Sometimes his fellow officers' sense of humor was enough to make Chad explode. He held to what was becoming a hair trigger temper and tossed the box of glow-in-the-dark condoms in the trash. Where he was headed, with whom, and why had made the rounds all over the department since he'd met with Morrison three days ago. He'd been smirked at, patted on the back in sympathy, and endured off-color remarks since the word went out that his undercover assignment was to move in with a Dom. Keeping smart-assed answer from alienating him with his peers had been an exercise in control.

"Chief wants to see you before you leave," Phillips informed him. As he walked off chuckling, he couldn't resist adding, "Don't let them get to you, son. Although better you than me. I'd look like hell in a cock cage."

"Just how is it you know what that even is?" Chad demanded.

"This case is giving me an education," Phillips called back. "You're going to get one hell of one too."

Chad didn't doubt that one fucking bit. Professor Morrison had the balls to email him a reading list, telling him to study the lifestyle before he appeared at his residence, along with the terse message to study well, treating him like one of his damn students.

How Chad felt about the situation must have shown. His chief took one look at him and shook his head. "You look ready to explode. Maybe you're not the right man for this assignment after all."

"I'll be fine once I get away from all these assholes and their asinine senses of humor. It's too late to call it off anyway. Morrison has already set the thing up, telling everyone I'm an old friend he reconnected with recently."

"Are you going to be able to do this?"

Chad blew out a breath. "Yeah, but you can bet your ass I'm not going to like it. The guy's a smug, arrogant ass."

15

"Feeling that way is going to make it pretty hard for you to pretend to be a boyfriend let alone a sub—if I've got that whole thing right."

"Nah, I got it covered. I'll keep my eyes down and my mouth shut. He'll do all the talking for me and tell me when and how to move every minute, according to the reading list he sent." He shook his head and gave a short laugh. "In private, I'll just stay away from him to keep from punching his lights out."

"If you think—"

Chad held his hand up to stop the chief's alarm. "I'm kidding. Sorry. I won't punch him," he said with a laugh. "I will stay away from him though, as much as possible. He irritates the hell out of me. Let's just hope this does put him on the top of the killer's hit list, and we get this over with quickly."

"I'll be at the funeral. If I see you're having trouble keeping in character, I'll pull the plug on you so fast your head will swim," he said in warning.

"I'll be fine." God, he wished he felt as confident as he sounded. He hadn't read much. He'd gotten tired of having a hard-on and having to jack off for relief.

* * * *

Chad pulled up to the house and whistled softly. The professor lived well. He certainly lived on a higher level than the studio apartment Chad crashed in when he dragged in exhausted from work every night. The house was a long, low-slung brick one story, sitting in the middle of a cul-de-sac. The neighborhood was a good one and very exclusive. After checking him out, Chad understood how he could afford the luxury. College professors didn't make the kind of money needed to support this life style. He'd come from a wealthy family as well as making a slight fortune on books he'd written, along with what he pulled in with lectures. The books were all about literary figures like Shakespeare and Marlowe and Donne, but written with a modern, popular appeal. One had even made the bestseller lists.

Pulling his old duffle bag from the back seat, he couldn't help enjoying the thought that his country boy manners might just be an embarrassment to the lofty professor.

Chad came from the small town of Dacula, only a short distance from Athens, but a world away in culture and refinement. His family was typical middle-class, his father a millworker and his mother a housewife. Chad had gone to school at the University as a night student to cut expenses, worked during the day to pay for it, and had never participated much in campus life. Adam—he had to get accustomed to calling him Adam, not Morrison—had been watching for him. He opened the door before Chad reached it.

"You're late. You'll have to hurry to change if we're going to be there on time."

"There's nothing wrong with what I have on for a funeral."

Adam, nattily dressed in a navy blue suit with a snowy white shirt and a tie in muted shades of red, gave him a once over, an eyebrow rising slightly. "There is. I've laid clothes out for you in the guest room. You're going to have to trust me to know the image you must project to make this work. You can't look like a cop. Hurry and get rid of the gun I told you to leave at home."

"Just what the hell kind of body guard would I be without a gun?" Chad shot back.

"Just how believable would you be as my sub carrying one?" Adam countered. "Leave it here. Here is where the danger exists, is it not?"

Gritting his teeth, Chad went where Adam directed. The interior of the house was as elegant as the exterior, full of dark woods and what seemed to Chad to be expensive antiques. The room he'd been given was bigger than his whole apartment. A tall four-post bed sat in the middle of the room, draped with dark brown covers. He didn't even want to set his bag down on the gleaming wood floors for fear he'd scratch or stain them somehow.

Seeing what was laid out for him, he had to admit, the clothes looked much better than what he had on. They should have for as much as he guessed the suit, shirt, shoes, and even socks must have cost. Definitely higher quality than Chad was used to. They fit him, too, and he was right. No way would the shoulder holster he'd switched to have been invisible under the jacket. Adam had a good eye, making Chad wonder how many men he measured by sight alone to buy clothes for. The black suit was slim cut and fit him like a glove. The shirt was charcoal, and the black, textured tie was silk. The shoes were expensive Italian loafers Chad was pretty sure cost more than his monthly salary. They must have belonged to the professor, because they were a little scuffed on the bottom. He kind of liked the idea of wearing shoes that belonged to Adam, and what the hell was wrong with him for even thinking like that?

"Satisfied?" he asked, rejoining Adam where he waited in the living room.

"More so than before." He straightened Chad's tie and tugged at the coat. "You'll do for off the rack. He looked down at his feet. Good. The shoes fit you. My young nephew left them here when he last visited. I thought they might do for you."

"Your nephew? How old is he?"

The professor smirked a little. "Fifteen. He's about your size."

Chad glared at him, but he was already turning away. "Come on. I'll drive." He led the way out the door, locking it behind him. "Remember when we get to the church, walk just at my heel. Did you read the books I instructed you to get?"

"Part of one." He felt like an idiot trailing along behind him like a well-trained puppy. "I don't have a lot of free time for reading."

"Chin up, eyes lowered. Watch where I walk."

Chad quickly dropped his eyes to Adam's feet. "Yeah, okay." Watching his feet really did help him to stay close by his side, but just a step behind.

Adam's next comment really raised Chad's hackles. Adam's head tipped to the side as he opened the passenger side door for Chad. "It's not as important outside the club, of course, but it will be good practice for you. I've told my friends you're in training, so if you mess up, it's not too big a deal."

"I'm not some damned dog."

"No, but you do need training. If anyone had overheard that comment, they would know immediately this is all an act. Watch your mouth. Bratty behavior is something I don't stand for, and my friends know it."

"How about you stop deliberately baiting me so the killer comes after us instead of some other innocent victims?"

"How about you let go of your macho posturing long enough to be a believable sub?" Adam countered. "Prove to me you can do it, before either of us get in a position where it could make a difference. Most things I can pull you out of, but if you don't follow my direction you could get yourself into a situation at the club I wouldn't be able to help you with. Some of the Doms there are what you'd call hardcore. If you're going to do this, then for God's sake take it seriously. It's not a game."

Chad glared at him a second before what he said processed. Adam was right. He dropped his eyes and even slumped his shoulders a bit. "I'm sorry. Uh, Master. I won't forget again."

"Oh good Lord, stand up straight and call me Sir. You're not a slave, just a sub, and I'm your Dom. Now that didn't hurt a bit, did it?" Adam asked with a slight smile. "Let's try to relax for the drive."

Letting go of his attitude actually hadn't hurt. Though he felt his pride should suffer to a degree, in a strange way, he didn't feel humiliated. Adam wore his dominance and authority like a cloak, and it seemed natural to give him the respect of the honorific. Chad slipped into the passenger seat and truly did relax. From this point on, it was up to Adam. He was just along for the ride, and all he had to do was keep his ears and eyes open when they got there. In a way, it took a lot of pressure off.

* * * *

The funeral proceedings were predictably solemn and sad. Two caskets sat in the front of the chapel, draped with flowers. The pews were full with many of the mourners in tears, both men and women. The pastor of some crazy church Chad had never heard of before gave a sermon on the grace of a loving God who accepted all men into his heart, sinners and saints. Chad wasn't too sure which the preacher applied to the deceased, but his words seemed to comfort the members of the families in the front pews.

"Who is he?" Chad whispered.

Adam leaned close. "Not now. I'll answer all your questions when we're in private again."

Chad wanted to whip back a sarcastic, "Yes, Sir," but held his tongue. His job there wasn't to catalog who was in attendance. The others from the department who were present would do that, comparing them to those who attended the other funeral, but he was curious. He reminded himself his job was to convince anyone who watched that he was Adam's submissive, maybe even especially Adam.

After the services, the families loaded into limousines for the trip to the cemetery. Waiting for them to leave, Chad tuned into a conversation between the pastor and some woman.

"I am so sorry. I know what a burden he is to you," she told him, her voice dripping in consolation.

"It is his home as much as mine," the pastor answered. "He is such a lost soul. I only wish I could help him."

"How long will he stay?"

"I've no idea. He comes and goes as he pleases, though I admit to hoping it won't be a long visit."

"It must be so hard for you."

"He is my brother. I would never turn him out, and I do always have hope that someday I may reach him."

Adam took his arm, tugging him away. "It's time to leave."

"What's that pastor's name?"

"Jason Rubin."

They got in the car, and Adam waited for Chad to put on his seat belt. A Dom handled his sub with care and protection, Chad reminded himself. He rolled his eyes as Adam slipped in behind the wheel. "What kind of church is this anyway?"

"A non-denominational church sympathetic to alternative lifestyles. Why?"

"Do you know anything about the pastor's brother?"

"Jeremy? No, not much. From what I gather, he's a n'eer-do-well who goes off chasing one scheme after another and returns when he's failed and broke. I've only met him briefly once. How did you know about him?"

"Overheard a conversation. How does the guy feel about gays?"

"No idea." Adam glanced at Chad quickly as he drove. "As I said, I only met him once, briefly, but his manner wasn't pleasant. You don't think—"

Chad waved the rest of his question away. "I don't think anything more at this point than he might be a person of interest. Who was the woman talking to the pastor?"

"Millie Grant. She's single, and the pastor's single. She never gives up trying."

"He's not interested?"

"He's taken a vow of celibacy even though the church doesn't require it of their pastors." His lips twisted into a grim smile. "He says he couldn't be a proper husband or father if there were children and continued to dedicate his life to the church. I suspect if he were to take a mate, though, it wouldn't be a woman."

"He's gay?" Chad nodded. "That makes sense. That explains why he's in a church for alternative life styles."

"Possibly, but he says it's because of his father. Jason makes no secret of his father's lifestyle. His father was gay, with a healthy dose of kink. The man died a few months ago. Jason had a difficult time dealing with it, fell into a depression, wouldn't leave his house for days. They didn't have a good relationship, but Jason said he had always hoped they would someday."

"You're close enough to him to know all that?" Chad asked, tucking away all the bits and pieces Adam gave him, making particular note of the mention of the time frame—two months, about the time when the killings started. Maybe Jason wasn't the only one adversely affected by the father's death.

"Everyone knows all of that. Jason's quite open about it. He's preached about it a few times."

"How old is this brother of his?"

"Two years older, I think, although they look enough alike to be twins, except for the disreputable way Jeremy keeps himself, unshaven, hair dirty and uncombed. There's no excuse in being slovenly." Stopping for a red light, Adam twisted in his seat to look at Chad. "The brother has really caught your interest."

"Yeah, he has. Has he ever worked at the University?"

"Not to my knowledge."

"Did all of the victims attend this church?"

"No, only the two buried today."

"But you do?"

"No, I'm in a support group at Jason's request for troubled young men whose families have difficulty accepting their sexual orientation. That's my only connection."

"Does the brother work at the church?"

"I believe he has at various times, but not consistently."

"What—hey, where the hell are you going?" Chad exclaimed, coming out of his train of thought enough to realize they were not driving to Adam's home.

"To the club in Atlanta."

Chad started and whipped his head around to face Adam. One hand gripped the arm rest and the other the seat edge. "It's the middle of the day!"

20

"Yes and attendance should be light this early. A good time to let you see the operation and meet the few who'll be there."

"Wait a damn minute!"

Adam did more than wait. He pulled over and stopped the car. "Is our association to end this soon?"

Furious over his panicked reaction and at Adam for goading him again, he didn't hold back his temper. "It's the first freaking day, and I've got things to do!"

Adam glanced at his watch. "What else do you have to do?"

Getting control of his voice, he spoke more calmly. "Go in to the office and start research on this brother for one thing."

Adam's voice remained mild. "As I understand it from my conversation this morning with your chief, your assignment is to stay with me—while I follow my normal patterns—and leave the field work to the other detectives assigned to the case. Isn't that correct?" He didn't wait for an answer. "I believe you could easily call in the information you've gathered to start them on research. Until then," he cast a wicked little sideways glance over at Chad, "you're all mine."

Chad steamed in silence, shocked at how the last comment gave him a funny little twisting sensation in his gut. He shoved it away, fuming over the fact Adam had been speaking with his chief. It felt a little like going behind his back, and he didn't appreciate it.

"Could it be that you're afraid of attending the club?" Adam asked, filling the silence.

"I'm not afraid." Curious, terrified, fascinated was more like it, though Chad was not going to admit to any of those things. "Okay, yes, it makes me uncomfortable. I thought I'd have a little more time to get used to the idea. You seem to take some kind of perverse pleasure in rubbing my nose in it."

"Not at all. Your chief said he wanted you to become immersed in the lifestyle. Let plenty of people see you as my sub. This is the only way to do it."

"I feel like you're deliberately trying to embarrass me."

Adam cut him off, his voice commanding and forceful without ever raising it. "Visiting this early presents a distinct advantage. As I stated before, attendance should be light this early in the evening, making your introduction to the club a little easier. It will also afford you the opportunity to meet several of those who attended the funeral, since there's a small wake planned in honor of the deceased. The decision was to have it there at the club where the victims found some pleasure, and we wouldn't embarrass the family at their function. This is just a private good-bye for us, many of whom did not attend the funeral."

"I get it."

With a smile of satisfaction, he added, "Then too, there's the matter of what you'll be wearing."

Chad glanced down at himself. "What I'm wearing? What do you mean?"

"Normally, my subs would be wearing a lot less, shall we say? Because of the occasion, that won't be expected tonight. It will help ease you into the scene a little as well as the events of the day giving us an excuse to leave early."

Chad groaned softly. "Why didn't you just say so and give me some warning?"

Putting the car back in gear and turning away, Adam smiled, "Because your reactions are so amusing I can't help myself." He slanted a look at Chad. "Predictable, but amusing."

"You're really enjoying this, aren't you?"

"I'm beginning to, yes. Make your phone call. It'll take us at least an hour to get there."

* * * *

It took almost an hour and a half because of traffic. It was close to seven o'clock when they arrived, and the parking lot was far from empty. "This is light attendance?"

Adam shrugged. "Sorry. Looks like I miscalculated a bit."

Chad shot him a furious look, and even before he got out of the car, he had to take several deep breaths to steel himself for what was coming. With only a vague idea of what he was going to see after his visits to some of the sites online, he hoped he wasn't going to humiliate himself with an unwanted arousal if they played one of the scenes he'd heard about or seen online. He'd planned on wearing baggy jeans during their visit to the club to hide his possible reaction, not these tightly tapered trousers. He should have known Adam would never let him get away with that. He was beginning to realize exactly how much control Adam would have.

Taking some solace in the length of the suit jacket, he had to drop his gaze in embarrassment and irritation when Adam made him remove his jacket and tie and unbuttoned most of the buttons on his shirt. If anyone saw the muscles in his jaw jumping from gritting his teeth, too damn bad.

"What, no collar?" Chad, his voice tight and pissed off, knew he was being a sarcastic ass, but he didn't care. He'd have to pretend to be meek and obedient soon enough. For now, he felt a little better expressing himself.

"You haven't earned one yet. You're supposed to be in training, remember? My friends aren't stupid, Chad. Drop this macho bullshit and straighten up. You'll have to at least try to role play. Otherwise you're just wasting my time."

Chad dropped his eyes. "I'm sorry. You're right."

"Good boy," Adam told him. "Now follow along behind me. Stand behind my chair and present yourself."

"Um…what?"

Adam turned am angry gaze up to his face. "Did you read any of the materials I suggested? This is basic stuff, Chad. Everything you do in there reflects on me. Do you understand that?"

The remark surprised and chastened Chad. People inside the club would be watching him, thinking he was Adam's sub. The sudden weight of responsibility landed on his shoulders. He had a job to do, one he'd sabotage if he didn't straighten himself up, and he found himself not wanting to embarrass Adam. After all, the department had gotten Adam into this, and Adam was trying to help. Chad squared his shoulders, determined to be the best sub he could be to impress the professor. He stood silently, fidgeting a little, but lowering his gaze and hunched his shoulders, trying to look like he thought a sub should look.

Adam blew out a long, irritated breath. "Okay, stand up straight. Clasp your hands behind your back. Good. Now spread your legs a little farther apart. Chin up, eyes down. Good." Adam walked around him, inspecting his posture before giving a curt nod. "Okay, I guess you'll do. Stand like that behind my chair, but first offer to get me a drink. After you bring it back, stand behind my chair in this position. Don't make eye contact with any of the Doms and let me do the talking. Got it?"

"I got it," he said quietly. "What if someone asks me something I don't know?"

"They shouldn't. As a general rule, other Doms don't speak to a sub without his Dom's permission, but you're not collared, so if you stray too far, someone might speak to you. If something like that should happen, just look to me. I'll keep an eye on you and help out. Now, are you ready?"

Chad nodded. "Then let's go."

The club looked to be a converted warehouse. A guard checked Adam's membership card and opened the door for them. Chad made a mental note to ask Philips if they knew guests were allowed in without identifying them. Inside, the music was loud, the lights were dim, and there seemed to be a good number of people inside, though there were also a lot of empty tables. A number of people were eating dinner and chatting. It seemed like any other club at first glance.

Males and females of various ages either sat at the tables or moved around the room. The club had a large dance floor and a long bar along the side. The lighting was low, like most every other club Chad had ever been to. As his eyes adjusted to the dimness, however, he saw the differences. Some of the men and women were wearing choker style necklaces, and a few were even wearing what looked like black or spiked dog collars.

Chad was at first shocked and then fascinated. A few people knelt on the floor next to their companions or leaned against their legs, while the people sitting at the tables seemed to mostly ignore them, except for an occasional pat on the head or off-hand caress. A couple of men and women were standing behind their companions, like Adam told Chad he was to do, all of them in the position Adam had just shown him. What was shocking to Chad was the way they were dressed...or undressed as the case may be. There was a great deal of leather and piercings, and one woman and a few of the men were totally nude. Some were wearing bikini briefs or jock straps, while a few he spotted even wore black leather hoods that completely covered their heads. Something else to mention that to the investigating team. Anyone could hide under one of those hoods.

He also noticed the huge mixture of social classes in the room. Some were like Adam, preppy and prosperous looking, while others seemed to have much rougher edges. He remembered Adam's warning about the hardcore Doms. It was easy to see what he'd meant. Some of these boys looked like they played rough.

Adam elbowed him in the side. "Don't stare. It's rude. Focus on me and pay attention. Stay at my heel."

Chad lowered his eyes immediately and started forward, only too happy to be following Adam and sticking close by him. Adam had become a familiar port in an alien sea. When Adam reached behind him and took Chad's hand, Chad's first instinct was to pull away. He forced himself to relax and realized he actually felt grateful.

Adam towed him to a table in the back and sat down, releasing his hand. Several men were already there, but before he could focus on them, Adam pulled him down toward him by putting a hand around the back of his neck. Speaking in his ear over the loud music, he said, "Bourbon on the rocks, Chad."

Chad stared at him blankly for probably a few seconds too long before he remembered he was supposed to get Adam a drink.

Chad nodded and hurried off to the bar to order Adam's drink for him. It took him a few minutes to get the attention of the bartender, but then he had his prize and began to carefully carry it back to the table. On the way back, he noticed another sub delivering a drink to his Dom He knelt beside him and held the drink up to him before settling back in a waiting position, still kneeling, but sitting back on his heels, his hands behind his back.

Realizing Adam had been going easy on him, Chad found himself wanting to impress him with how quickly he could learn. When he got to their table, he sank to his knees beside Adam and held the drink up like an offering.

Surprise and pleasure leap in Adam's eyes, and he smiled. "Thank you, Pet."

A voice from across the table startled Chad.

"Well, Adam, he's very pretty, but I didn't think you liked gingers."

Gingers? Chad made an unconscious movement, and Adam pressed his

24

shoulder back down. "Settle down, baby."

Sitting back, Chad heard a little tsking noise from Adam and realized his posture was bad. Remembering the boy he'd seen on his way back to the table, he mimicked him, knees apart, back straight with his hands locked behind him. Adam rewarded him by running his fingers over his hair.

"I wouldn't say that," Adam said softly. "Besides, Chad's hair is lovely."

"So you're training a new sub? I didn't think that was your preference," another voice said to Chad's left.

Adam's voice was silky smooth as he answered. "Only with someone truly special. As you can see, he is."

The talk became more general then, thank God, and the men at the table continued with their dinners. With the attention not focused on him, he allowed himself to surreptitiously scan the men at their table, listening absently to their conversations. There were four of them, all fairly young, mostly dressed in suits, like Adam, as they'd just come from the funeral services. Only one was wearing leathers. Three subs knelt beside their Doms as well, though they were across the table. All four Doms appeared to be in their thirties, from early to middle, their subs from middle twenties to maybe early thirties. He didn't miss the fact everyone at the table fit into the victims' profiles.

"Rubin is pretty nervy for a preacher," one commented, catching Chad's attention. "He didn't come right out and hit me up for a donation today, but promised me he'd be in touch."

"It is a worthy cause," said another of the men.

"I won't debate that, but I get tired of his almost constant requests for donations. The minute he shows up, I get out my checkbook just to get rid of him."

The conversation lapsed as a server brought Adam a plate, and Chad's stomach growled. It was getting late, and he'd been too nervous to eat much lunch. He'd missed meals before when he was busy on a case and didn't have time to stop, but he'd been active then, not just sitting around, or in this case, kneeling. He was wondering how much longer to would have to wait to eat when Adam held out a small piece of a sandwich in front of his mouth. He was so startled he jumped a little, and Adam's other hand fell lightly on the back of his neck. He shook the piece of sandwich in front of Chad's mouth slightly, and Chad got the hint, trying to take it with his hand. The sandwich was pulled away. Chad looked up in surprise.

Adam was giving him a stern look. "I didn't tell you to move your hands, Chad. Open your mouth."

He put his hands behind his back quickly. The sandwich piece reappeared. He opened his mouth, and the piece was placed on his tongue. It was some kind of ham and cheese, and as hungry as he was, it tasted absolutely delicious. He sat happily chewing until another piece appeared, and he opened his mouth again. He got a sudden mental picture of how he would look if any of the guys from work could see him, but mentally shrugged. None of them were here, while he was starving and playing a part.

Adam eventually fed him what must have been an entire sandwich, and he ate every bite, even taking sips of Adam's water when he held it down to Chad's lips. The entire operation was surprisingly intimate, and when the meal was over and Adam pulled him over to rest against his leg, he went willingly and without even thinking about it. He realized he hadn't really been totally aware of his surroundings since he'd begun eating from Adam's hand and reminded himself to focus.

The man across the table from them was speaking again. "My sub and I are doing a scene in a few minutes. Are you going to display your new boy tonight, Adam?"

"No, not tonight. He's not ready," Adam answered.

"I'd be glad to lend a hand in his training, Adam," came a voice from across the table. "We could take him to a private room."

Chad glanced up to see the man wearing leathers was the one who'd made the comment. He was balding, though probably only in his mid-thirties, and had a slight paunch. Chad didn't find him the least bit attractive, certainly not as attractive as Adam. Since Adam hadn't replied, the words came out of Chad's mouth before he even thought about it. "He doesn't need any help from you."

A small silence fell over the table, and the Dom in leathers gave Adam an incredulous look before he turned a furious glare on Chad.

Adam looked down at him. "Your behavior just demonstrated how unready you are." Adam said sternly. He leaned over and took Chad's chin in his hand. "Now be quiet."

Chad blew out a long, frustrated breath. Even knowing damn good and well he shouldn't argue with Adam, words spilled out of his mouth. "I only said—"

Adam cut him off, his lips white with anger. "I heard what you said, damn it. As a matter of fact, just go away."

Chad's head jerked up to look at him. "Huh?"

"Go away. I'm not pleased with you right now. Go mingle or observe or whatever and come back when you think you can behave yourself."

Hot anger and embarrassment flooded him, and Chad rose to his feet awkwardly, stiff from being on his knees for so long. Come back when he could behave himself? Damn him. He glanced around at the faces of the others at the table. The subs all looked a little horrified, but the Doms, or whatever they were, seemed amused. Fuck them and fuck Adam.

"Okay, I will," he said and marched off across the room, turning his back on all of them. Once he'd gotten a few steps from the table, he realized he didn't have a clue as to what to do with himself. Well, first things first, he needed to find a bathroom. He located one down a dim hallway and went inside to use a stall. Just whipping it out at the urinal in a club like this made him uncomfortable. Maybe afterward, he'd go get himself a drink and sit at the bar for a while and just observe. Observe what, he wasn't too sure, but he'd be damned if he'd go back over to Adam's table. He'd just dismissed him, like he was badly behaved child. Arrogant asshole.

He came out of the stall and washed his hands. Two men stood at the urinals, both giving him a good look over with interest. They were older than Chad, both maybe in their forties, and looked a little like biker dudes, with their leather and tatts. One of them nudged the other when Chad came out of the stall, and the smile he gave Chad was friendly, if a little predatory. "Hey there, sweet thing, all alone?"

"Um, yeah, I guess I am." Some part of Chad's brain, the logical, reasoning, cop instinct part, told him to get away from these guys. They were bad news, and he did not want to start up something and draw attention to himself. The other part of his brain, the hurt, pissed off part, wanted to hit something. If these two wanted to start something, he'd be ready.

"Really?" He tilted his head. "Would you like to play some? We could show you a good time."

"No, I'm just here to watch tonight."

The biggest one finished and came over to stand beside him. "Watching can be fun, but a boy like you looks like he has a lot to learn, and we'd be glad to teach you."

"That's right," said the other one. "We have a room in back. Come with us and we'll take good care of you."

"I don't think so," Chad said, shrugging off the hand on his arm. "Leave me the fuck alone." He glared at both of them and stepped quickly away, back out into the hallway. One of the men from Adam's table headed into the bathroom just then and slipped past him, shooting him a look of amusement, and once again, the underlying anger Chad felt all the time anymore bubbled to the surface, looking for a way out.

A voice spoke up behind him. The two guys from the bathroom had followed him out. "Are you sure you won't change your mind? I think you need a little loosening up, sweetheart. I can do that for you."

Chad turned and swung out blindly. His fist was caught in an iron grip and twisted around behind his back. Before he could move away, the other hand was wrestled back to join it, and cold metal snapped around his wrists. He'd been cuffed and expertly, too. When he opened his mouth to yell, one man forced a rubber ball into his mouth while the other held him. Attached straps were wrapped around the back of his head before he could even try to spit it out and jerked tight to hold the ball in his mouth. Chad's teeth sank down into the rubber, and he almost gagged. They took him by his arms and pulled him down to one of the doors leading off the hall. Chad wasn't very big, but he was pretty strong. Those two were something else. It was impossible to stop them or protect himself with his hands secured behind his back. Even his shouts came out as garbled nonsense. They dragged him inside the room and over to a bed in the middle of the floor. Pushing him to a seated position on the bed, they shoved him back down when he tried to get up. Chad had a very bad feeling this was not going to end well—at all.

* * * *

Adam jiggled his knee nervously and wondered where the hell Chad had gotten to. He'd been frustrated and angry—and he had to admit, disappointed. Needing to show his displeasure to his friends avidly watching their exchange, he'd sent Chad away, but he was uneasy. Chad could get himself into a lot of trouble very easily in this place. The young detective had no idea what he was dealing with. Adam thought he could keep an eye on him and make sure he didn't get himself into any trouble, but he'd lost sight of him and was worried.

His intention had been to teach him to stay quiet when they were at the club with a kind of time out. Instead the little fool had been angry and taken off for the bathrooms where Adam couldn't watch out for him.

The club was unusually busy for that hour on a Friday, and it seemed like many people had decided to start their evening early. In addition, some of the hard core Doms were in attendance, and it wouldn't do for Chad to fall in range of their radar, especially un-collared and alone. They wouldn't be able to resist his sweet little straight boy looks, and he could get himself in way too deep with the wrong guys. Cole, one of his friends at the table, noticed his uneasiness and told him quietly he'd check on him when he left to go to the bathroom.

Almost five more minutes passed, and Adam was about to look for Chad himself when his friend reappeared and came straight over to Adam to whisper in his ear. "Better go check on your boy, Adam. He was standing in the hallway when I went in, but when I came back out I saw him being hustled down the hall to a room by O'Brien and Parker."

"Shit." Adam threw his napkin down on the table and got up quickly, turning to his friend. "Which room?"

"Last one on the hall by the bathrooms. Need me to get one of the dungeon masters?"

"No, I'll handle it."

He said the last words over his shoulder as he was on the move, afraid of what might be happening in that room already. O'Brien and Parker were regular players at the club. Parker was a tough, sadistic Dom, and O'Brien was a switch, his sometime partner. They were known for picking up new boys in the club and also for their harsh treatment of the subs they played with. Of course, the subs had their safe words, and the scenes he'd witnessed had never gotten out of hand, but who knew what might go on behind the closed doors of a private room.

If he were to salvage this thing and not blow Chad's cover, he needed to see if he could extricate Chad by himself and not involve club management. Word got around quickly in this place, and if Chad flashed a badge or said the wrong thing, the whole plan was over before it even got started.

Moving down the corridor, he paused outside the last door and listened through the wood panels. No screaming, which was a good sign. He rapped sharply on the door and not waiting for an answer, stepped inside.

Chad was stripped naked and lying flat on his stomach on the bed. He wasn't moving. Both Doms stood over him and looked up at Adam in surprise as he came in the door. One of them held a whip, and a flogger was laid out on the bed, ready to be used next.

"What the fuck, Morrison?" O'Brien snarled at him. "Get your own boy."

Adam nodded toward the bed. "That is my boy, and I didn't give you permission to play with him."

The bigger of the two men, Parker, turned toward Adam aggressively. "He's not collared. He said he was alone, and he came willingly. He never said he belonged to you."

"Regardless of that fact, he does. You know the rules of the club, Parker. You too, O'Brien, and he doesn't look too willing to me." He nodded toward Chad, who had begun to move his hips a little, thrusting into the bed, humping it. His hands were bound behind his back and straps, no doubt holding a gag in place, were buckled behind his head. He looked vulnerable and alone, and Adam's heart almost stopped in his chest. He had to get him out of here in one piece, no matter what it took.

Adam's gaze fell on an empty glass siting on the table by the bed. "Fuck, did you drug him, asshole? Why is he humping the bed like that?"

"We gave him a little drink just to loosen him up. If he took drugs before he got in here, I have no way of knowing. Maybe someone slipped him a roofy."

Chad moaned, thrusting at a frantic pace and rubbing his groin on the mattress.

"Yeah or maybe you gave him one. Damn it, Parker, what did you give him?"

"Nothing much. Just something mild to loosen him up, like I said. He was too uptight. He was waiting for us in the hallway. I thought he just liked to fight, and this would calm him down so he didn't hurt himself."

"Calm him, my ass." Adam gave Parker a dirty look and crossed over to Chad, sitting beside him. He took off the gag first. Chad coughed and turned his head slowly to look at him. His eyes were red and his pupils were blown. He swallowed hard a few times and finally managed to speak. "Adam, h-help me."

Adam's chest tightened. He rubbed Chad's back and spoke soothingly to him. "I'm here, baby boy. Just calm down."

"What-what's happening to me? God, I feel so…" He humped again with loud groan.

Adam turned back to the two men. He wanted to smash their faces but forced himself to be calm. If he was to get them both out of this in one piece, without alerting anyone to what was happening, he had to play his cards right. "The boy belongs to me. I might let you watch, but that's it. Nobody touches him but me."

O'Brien grabbed his crotch through a slit in his leather gear and stroked himself. "Watching sounds good to me."

Parker nodded, and the two of them stationed themselves at the foot of the bed. Adam had to think fast to come up with something to show his domination over Chad, but not harm him, physically or mentally. Despite his teasing, he had intended to respect Chad's boundaries and not do anything to him that would compromise him in any way. They had to put on a show to get out of here peacefully, and Adam had to figure out what to do to mitigate the damage to Chad as much as possible. He turned back to the two men. "Uncuff him."

Parker stepped over and produced a key, taking off heavy, leather cuffs quickly. Adam rolled the boy over on his back and knelt on the bed beside him, bending down low and speaking in his ear. To the men standing close by, it might have sounded like endearments.

"Chad, can you focus on me?" Chad raised his eyes to gaze blearily at him. "Do you trust me?"

He nodded slowly, grabbing at himself and groaning. "Pay attention," Adam said. "You have to do whatever I tell you to, okay? Don't question, don't complain, just do it."

Another nod and Adam sat up on his knees next to him. "Make yourself come for us, baby. Show us what you got."

Chad's eyebrows rose, but his hand floundered to find and close around his dick. Uncoordinated because of the drugs, he had trouble accomplishing it. Adam helped him by taking Chad's hand and wrapping his fingers around his shaft, using his own hand to hold it there. He began stroking him up and down, keeping eye contact until Chad finally seemed to understand what it was he was supposed to do. He fell into a rhythm then, and though jerky and unfocused, it seemed to be getting the job done. Chad's eyes rolled back in his head, and he moaned and whimpered.

"Good boy," Adam said, cupping his balls and knead them gently. "Come for me, baby. Keep your eyes on me and come just for me. You know you want to."

Chad whimpered again and tried to hide his face against Adam's knee. Adam threaded his fingers through his hair tenderly. "Come for me, sweetheart. Come for me and then I'm going to turn you over my knee and spank you so hard you'll never get yourself into a mess like this again."

Chad stiffened, and he turned his head back to stare at Adam, his pupils blown. His breath hitched, and then he came, spurting all over himself, yelling with surprise, throwing his head back and baring his teeth. Spent, he slumping back down on the bed, his chest rising and falling rapidly. He looked up at Adam and whimpered.

Adam smiled, his hand tracing a lazy pattern on Chad's chest. "So you like that idea? You like the idea of lying across my lap and feeling helpless and controlled? Do you want my hand pounding down on your ass until you can't think anymore and all you can do is beg me to stop?"

Chad shivered and gazed up into his eyes. "God, yes," he said, his words slurring, but with a look of yearning and trust on his upturned face.

* * * *

Chad watched Adam pull a condom over his dick within seconds and with surprising ease. He reached out to help, but Adam pushed his hand away with impatience, and heaved Chad's body over onto his lap, seemingly without effort. Adam was a big guy, but Chad had no idea he was that strong. He positioned Chad so he was lying across his lap, his ass in the air, his cock pressed down between Adam's thighs. Chad was still disoriented and things took on a dream-like quality, where he wasn't sure what was real and what was just imagined. He thought, for example, that he had just agreed to be spanked by Adam. Spanked. By Adam. He groaned again and tried to push himself up, but the dizziness kept him reeling, and a firm hand on his back kept him in place.

The room spun around him. He almost smiled at the crazy dream and rubbed his prick against Adam's thigh. Damn, it felt so good. It was a complete shock when Adam's hand came down hard on his bare ass, almost lifting him up off his thighs. Even though he vaguely knew it was coming, the pain was intense and to his horror, his eyes filled with tears even as his dick started to fill out. His body wanted to fuck something, to buck against the hold Adam had on his dick with his thighs, the friction and the sting in his ass feeling so good to his cock. Adam's hand came down again twice in rapid succession, and Chad cried out and reared up, only to be pushed back down again while two ghost-like figures in the room watched, both of them with their flies open, jacking off. Was this some kind of public scene they were doing?

It was all cloudy and confusing, and the only reality was the rub of Adam's pants against his rigid, sensitive cock and the force of his hand as it fell on

31

his ass again and again. The sting on his ass was the only thing that gave him a sense of reality. He bucked and cried out, frantically reaching around behind him for Adam's touch. Adam had become his only anchor, the only person he could count on or hang onto. Adam's hand met his and gripped it tightly, though his other hand was still planted in the small of his back, holding him firmly down. Adam leaned and crooned to him.

"Such a good boy. It will be over soon, and you can thank me. Put your hands back down now like a sweet boy and take the rest of your spanking for me. That's right. Lie still now."

The hand came down again and again, and each strike on his ass made his cock that much harder, though hot tears were by now streaming down his face. The hand stilled for a moment and rubbed his scorched ass, kneading the muscles and making him whimper.

"You want to come for me again, baby?"

"Y-Yes," he mumbled, not feeling quite so confused and dizzy anymore, but still so aroused. Chad didn't think he could come again so soon even in a dream, but his dick seemed to have other ideas. The orgasm come over him powerful and strong. The hand fell once more.

"Then come," he ordered.

Chad strained and cried out. He wanted to obey Adam desperately. His legs went stiff, and his hips still tried to find something to hump against. The hand around his waist lifted, and he slid off Adam's lap and onto the floor. Shuddering through the aftershocks of his orgasm, he suddenly felt cold, though his butt felt like it was on fire. In a crazy way he liked that he could still feel where Adam's hands had been on him, and he knew he'd feel it for days.

Adam asked where his clothes were, and then pulled off the used condom and lifting him to the bed. He spent some time putting Chad's arms in his sleeves. Chad had gone limp and had trouble helping him. He tried, but Adam pushed his fumbling hands away, buttoned his shirt, and then guided his feet into his pants legs. He lay back on the bed while Adam pulled up his pants, zipped, and buttoned them. Adam shoved his shoes on, pulled Chad to his feet, and looped his arm around his neck.

The next thing he knew he was being dragged outside in the cool night air, and when did it get so dark outside? He was having trouble walking so the guy at the door took one arm and Adam another as they half walked, half dragged him to the car. They sat him in the seat and, goddamn, his ass was sore. Adam buckled him in, and he heard him talking to the guard, but didn't understand anything they said.

Then there was wind in his face, and he turned his head to see Adam lit up by the dash lights. He reached for him, and Adam caught his fingers up and squeezed them. "Go back to sleep. I've got you." And that was the last thing he was aware of for a long time.

☐

3

Chad slept all the way home, no doubt due to the drugs he'd taken. Adam checked his pulse several times on the way home and found it strong and steady. He thought about driving to the nearest hospital, but Chad was asleep, his breathing more normal, and he wouldn't want any of this to get out, as it surely would if he took him to the ER.

When he got to his house, he drove into the garage and closed the door behind them, to be certain the detectives out there doing surveillance didn't see Chad being supported to get inside. They might have been helpful in handling him, but Chad would never live it down. He took him in the garage entrance, determined to deal with it himself. Damn it, he should never have let Chad out of his sight.

By the time they were inside, Chad roused a little and was able to walk with an arm around Adam to the guest room. He sat down on the side of the bed, and Adam helped him slip off his shirt. Since his underwear had been lost somewhere along the way, Adam left him in his pants, pulled the blanket over him and left him to sleep it off. Before he could go, however, Chad reached for his hand.

"Don't leave me."

With the size of his pupils still enormous, Adam doubted Chad knew where he was. The lost sound of his plea got to Adam though. Taking off his jacket and shoes, Adam lay down beside Chad on top of the blanket and put an arm around him, intending to stay with him only until he went to sleep. When the detective became fully aware of what had happened tonight, he was going to be furious, not to mention humiliated. It was better for all concerned if he woke up alone. Still, it wouldn't hurt to stay with him for a while, just to make sure he didn't have any ill effects from the drugs.

Chad was restless, pushing back into him and turning in his arms. He burrowed his face into the hollow between Adam's neck and his chest.

"Shit," Adam said quietly. He hadn't expected to feel so much tenderness for the younger man.

Chad's breathing evened out, and Adam eased over to his back to stare at the ceiling. This was not anything he was looking for. Chad was younger by close to ten years and confused about his sexuality, not even willing to admit he was gay, let alone into any kind of kink. Adam had thought at first it might be fun to tease and play with the handsome detective, but this had officially gone way too far. Adam had come to realize they were both in way over their heads, a hell of a thought to go to sleep with.

* * * *

When Adam awoke, sunlight streamed through the window. He sat up and looked over at Chad lying on his back, softly snoring. Easing off the bed, he picked up his shoes and jacket and went down the hall to the master suite. After showering and dressing in old jeans and a polo, he was starving and made his way to the kitchen to cook breakfast.

Though he only rarely ate eggs and bacon, he knew Chad would probably be hungry when he woke up. He fried some bacon, scrambled some eggs, and was on his second cup of coffee when he heard Chad coming down the hall and into the big open-plan living area. Chad stood just inside the door and glared furiously over at Adam where he sat at the table calmly sipping his coffee.

He looked surprisingly good after the rough night he'd had. A little pale, though, and he needed a shave. He hadn't showered yet, and still wore the suit pants he'd slept in and nothing else. Adam let his gaze roam over the broad expanse of muscled chest as Chad continued to give him an evil look.

"Good morning, Detective. I hope I didn't wake you up."

Chad took one step closer. His hands were clenched by his sides. "What the fuck happened last night?"

"Maybe you'd better sit down."

Chad glowered at him. "That's just it. I fuckin' can't sit down! My head hurts like hell, I ache all over, and my damn ass feels like it's on fire. I don't remember anything past thinking I needed to go to the bathroom. What did you do to me?"

Adam took another sip of coffee and considered carefully what he was going to say. If it hadn't been for the fact that when Chad came farther into the room, he could see him trembling, he might have been angry at his tone. As it was, he knew Chad was feeling vulnerable, confused, and transferring all those negative feelings into anger. He decided to cut him some slack.

"You got yourself in a little trouble last night. I got you out of it the best way I could. The least invasive way I could. Do you understand?"

"Hell no. You're going to have to spell it out for me. What the hell happened? Why can't I remember?"

Adam sat back in his chair and nodded toward the sofa. "Grab one of those pillows, bring it over here, and have a cup of coffee. I'll explain everything after you've eaten." He held up a hand when Chad started to protest. "No, you need some food inside you before we talk. It will help your headache."

Chad stood for another few seconds before stomping over to the couch and jerking up a pillow. He threw it in a chair and then eased himself down on it, wincing a bit and shooting another vicious look at Adam. Ignoring him, Adam filled a plate and poured him a cup of coffee. "Eat," he ordered and sat back down to watch him.

After only a few seconds' hesitation, Chad shoveled in the eggs and bacon and cleaned his plate in no time. Adam watched him with amusement. If Adam ate like that, he'd weigh three hundred pounds in no time, but Chad's abs were washboard slim. He must be even younger than Adam first thought. "How old are you?"

"Twenty-six," he answered between bites.

"You look younger."

Chad shrugged the comment off. When he finished his second helping and sat back in his chair, still glaring, Adam leaned forward, putting one elbow on the table. "Feeling better?"

Chad nodded curtly. "Now talk."

"What would you like to talk about first? The way you totally ignored everything I told you about being quiet and respectful in front of my friends?"

"You told me to go away."

Adam saw what looked like hurt in Chad's eyes, though Chad quickly hid it by looking down and pushing his plate away. "I had to be firm with you, or the people sitting at my table would never have believed you were training to be my sub. They know I don't like brats and would never allow my sub to speak up like that."

"Okay, I see that, I guess. Sorry, but I was defending you or trying to."

"I don't need defending, and I take care of my sub, not the other way around. I had to send you away to end things quickly and avoid either of us being goaded into an argument that would have made our actual relationship all too obvious."

"Then why didn't you—"

Adam held up a hand again. "That was an experienced Dom you were talking to, and you could have gotten in way over your head if I'd felt the need to punish you to satisfy him. I know, I know, you trust me not to hurt you, and I wouldn't, at least not physically, but I have no idea about your emotional state or what might be going up here." He tapped his temple. "Until I know exactly how you're going to react to everything I do to you, I can't risk your safety by being trapped into a situation that could have gotten out of hand. Until you have some real training, you need to keep your mouth shut and let me handle things."

Chad was quiet, staring down at the table top. "Okay. Now tell me how I got this sore ass if you didn't give it to me."

Adam permitted himself the slightest smile. "I did give it to you."

Chad's head popped up, and his mouth fell open. Adam sighed. "You went into the bathroom after you left the table and got yourself involved somehow with two Doms."

"Two...?" Chad's pupils nearly exploded.

Adam touched his hand to reassure him. "They didn't touch you...at least not the way you're obviously thinking. They did cuff your hands behind you and force some kind of date rape drug down your throat somehow. I think it was dissolved in a drink they gave you. Anyway, by the time I found you, you were stripped naked, face down, and gagged on a bed in a private room."

Chad's face drained of any color it might have regained. "Oh, shit."

"Oh, shit, indeed. They were about to have their way with you, I'm afraid. I did the only thing I could to stop them and not involve the management. If the dungeon masters had come in, they would have called the cops, and then everyone would have known exactly in what condition they found you—including your co-workers."

"Oh hell no!"

"Yes, that's how I thought you might feel."

"So...if you didn't call for help—who are the dungeon masters anyway?"

"They're identified by the black hoods they wear."

The one Chad noticed didn't look big enough to be a bouncer, but he was too distracted to want to comment. "Since you didn't call them, how did you get us out of there? Did you...?"

"No, I didn't. I gave them a show without going that far. With the drug working on you, I was able to make you masturbate while they watched."

Chad covered his face with both hands and groaned. Even the tips of his ears turned bright pink. Adam gave him a few moments to absorb the information before he pulled Chad's hands down.

"Look," Adam said, tipping his chin up with one finger. "At least it was your own hand, right?" He thought it best not emphasize how all three of them watched, or mention that the other two men in the room jerked themselves off to it. That was too much detail in Chad's currently fragile state.

"Okay," Chad said. "I hate the idea of it, but you're right. At least it was my own hand and not..." He shuddered. "Right. Thanks, Adam, that was quick thinking."

"You're welcome," Adam said, the corners of his mouth twisting up a little.

"But that still doesn't explain…uh…"

"Your sore ass? That would be from the spanking I gave you."

Chad sputtered a few times, and his face went to an alarming shade of red. "W-What did you say?"

"Chad, I had to give them some kind show to watch besides you jerking yourself off. I didn't want to use their flogger or the whip they had out ready to use on you."

"Oh, my God."

Adam continued, "I put you over my lap and gave you a spanking. You asked for it, actually, and came again in the process."

Chad jumped up from the table so fast, the chair fell to the floor behind him. He gave Adam an unreadable look and stormed from the room. Adam heard the guest room door slam and shook his head. He wondered if Chad was aware of how big an erection he had when he took off out of the room.

* * * *

Images from the night before began flooding back in Chad's head while Adam talked. His face burned with embarrassment with each disjointed one. Chad coped by hiding—and he admitted to himself he was hiding—in the guest room after he showered and dressed in his own clothes. He'd never been more humiliated in his life. His only consolation was that it could have been worse. Someone other than the arrogant Adam Morrison could have witnessed his disgrace. Knowing he was foolish to be furious with Adam over what he'd caused himself didn't help. He'd failed the role he'd taken on, gotten himself drugged, and nearly raped all because he had to open his big mouth and assert his macho pride instead of playing the role he'd sworn he'd play. He'd fucked up. Along with that were those flashes of disturbing memories that had him nursing a hard-on along with his sore ass.

In an effort to take his mind off the events of the night before, he called into the office for a report on the preacher and his brother. Phillips told him Jason Rubin had such a clean record he probably squeaked when he walked. The man had never even gotten a parking ticket. His brother, Jeremy, however, looked better and better as a suspect. He'd managed not to end up in jail, but he did have an assault charge against him two years ago that he'd skated on when the victim refused to press charges. It made him a prime candidate for the murders.

"Jeremy Rubin showed up here again around three months ago, only a month before the murders started. He comes and goes, traveling around, taking whatever job he can find," Philips said. "It doesn't look like he's held any job more than six months ever."

"None at the University or club?"

"Nope, but just like you said, he fits the profile the department shrink drew up for us, and he does hate gays. We may have verified that. Some people at his brother's church say he's made derogatory remarks, but we can't tie him directly to any of the victims. The church tie is too indirect. No real BDSM link. The focus of this killer is not on all gays in general, but on a specific segment of that population. BDSM includes women too, of course, but no women have been victims. The only definite links we have so far are men into BDSM connected to the University."

"Who have a lover," Chad added.

"Yeah, that too."

"This Jeremy worked off and on at the church. That ties him close enough to two of the victims for me. Start digging. There's got to be some connection between him and the other victims. I don't suppose there are any open warrants on him here so we could pick him up?"

"No and the chief doesn't want to alert him to our interest yet, not until we can get more to hang him with."

"Has he ordered any surveillance on him?"

"Not yet. He says the DA would have a fit with no more than we've got, no real probable cause."

"Shit. He won't give you the go ahead for anything, phone records, financial statements, nothing?"

"Too circumstantial. A judge won't clear us for any of that until we can come up with more."

"These killings have all the earmarks of a hate crime. The story I got is the guy hates his father because he deserted his family to live as an openly gay man. Even the timing with his father's death ties in as a trigger that set him off. What the hell more do they want before they untie our hands?" Chad demanded, his voice rising in anger.

"Evidence. The guy looks good for it with his record even though it's all minor crap and what Morrison told you about him, but none of it's concrete. We need to flesh it out some more before we move." He cleared his throat and asked, "How did your first day as a pet go?"

"I failed my paper training," he retorted bitterly, flushing with embarrassment and damned glad he was on the phone, not face to face for Philips to see it. "And they're called submissives, dumbass. But no, I didn't do so hot. Adam had to send me away from him in disgrace to cover my screw up."

Philips chuckled. "Hang in there. If this lead pans out, you could be out of there soon. I hear the professor can be a real prick."

"Not really. He's been nice enough so far. He did cover my ass last night." In more ways than one. The reminder had a strange effect on Chad. His damn prick renewed interest, and he squirmed with embarrassment, but the idea gave him a weird feeling of excitement at the same time. "Keep me in the loop. I'll call in if I get anything more. One thing you can do—research his father. Proving he was gay and a Dom could strengthen the motive link, if we could prove Jeremy harbored anger and resentment over it. Another thing, search the ViCAP for similar crimes. That might tell us where he's been going."

"Already got the computers running on that one. One thing you need to know, the captain is considering calling the FBI in if we don't get some results soon from your undercover gig. There's no damn doubt we've got a serial killer on our hands. Even though the chief's been stalling them, he'd rather lose control of the case than have any more deaths. If you can think of a way to draw more attention, I suggest you do it."

He disconnected with that gem, setting Chad's mind in motion. He walked out, found Adam in the living room and announced, "You need to take me to school."

"Excuse me?" he asked, looking up from the papers in his lap he was working on.

"Your classes. Our relationship needs more exposure. We've been seen together at the church and the club. The only other link, and the only one to both the attacks, is the University."

"I cannot think of a single valid reason to take you to work with me."

"I could show up for lunch."

"No."

"Why the fuck not? Didn't any of your boyfriends ever join you for lunch?"

"None of my subs, no. I understand you're upset about last night, but it only proved what I've been telling you, you are not trained enough for any long exposure in pretending to be my sub." He put down his pen and rubbed his forehead. "Not at the University, but maybe I could take you to one of my sessions with students at the church. It would be a more relaxed atmosphere than the club."

"Yeah, I could do that," Chad said eagerly.

"You need to train first. I don't want you embarrassing me again. Other friends of mine, who are also Doms, help me with the sessions, and we usually come back here afterwards for a drink. You'd have to serve us, and I may as well warn you now, you wouldn't be fully clothed. If you can't accept that, you'd only fail again."

Chad's face felt like it was on fire. He shot an accusing glare at Adam. "You shouldn't have taken me to that fucking club so soon."

Adam released a slow breath. He still used a soft tone, but firmness crept in. "I knew it was a risk, but we'd already been seen at the church. After I received the invitation, it would have seemed odd if I hadn't gone or if I had and not taken you. Not to go would have been—"

"I know all that shit!"

"Enough, Chad. I won't be yelled at in my own home."

"Or what? You going to spank me again?"

"Is that what you want?" he asked softly.

"Fuck no!" He paused and snarled, "Sir!"

"Don't call me that unless you mean it. We're not in a scene, and using the term signals your willingness to submit to me. We both know you're a long way from that. If you wish for this to continue, watch your tone. I won't stand for your disrespect. What do you want, Chad? Or do you even know?"

"I want this case solved and that murdering bastard locked up!" What he wanted to do at that moment was hit something—maybe even someone. His temper had been on edge for weeks, his ass ached, and he was damned good and well aware Adam knew he was standing there with a hard-on even before he spoke.

"You need to release some of that tension, Chad, or you're going to explode." He laid aside his papers. "Men in your profession need a release valve to keep from—"

"Don't start telling me something you don't know anything about," Chad told him coldly.

"I know a gay man when I see him," he said, looking Chad up and down slowly. "One way is to watch his eyes. There's a certain look a gay man gives another man, a kind of focused attention. Most straight men don't catch another man's gaze and hold it in that way."

"You're saying I'm gay?"

The professor shrugged, and Chad swallowed down the angry words he wanted to yell at him. Did he do what Adam just described? Had he done it when he first met Adam? As usual, Chad's mind skittered away from facing the idea he might be gay. He changed the subject. "I fucked up last night. If it ever gets out, I'll never be able to live it down."

"It will never leave the club. All the members have an unspoken mutual agreement to keep what happens there private, and yes, you did, as you say, fuck up."

"We've got a week for me to learn about all this before we go back to the club. I'd like to practice with this meeting of yours. I want to learn how to do it right. Can we do that?"

"Practice, you mean? Sure." The teasing smile was back on his face. "Come over here and sit down."

"I'm not doing real well with sitting today, thank you."

"Your discomfort will remind you what happens when you disobey," Adam said, a slight, teasing smile on his lips.

Chad didn't move.

"Or we can call this entire thing off right now. I have never been a patient man, and if you rebel against everything I tell you to do, you're wasting my time."

Grumbling under his breath, Chad crossed the room and stood, glaring down at him. "What you would do with your sub in the privacy of your home is not what I need to learn."

Adam blew out an exasperated breath. "Of course it is. You have to learn the process. What you need to learn is to obey me without argument, without question. Damn it, this has to become familiar enough to you that it's second nature. Anyone with any knowledge of the lifestyle could spend five minutes in a room with us and know this is a sham. If you want this killer to notice us—and believe we're a couple—you have to learn more. I need to train you enough that you can carry this off believably by acting the way you should without even having to think about it."

Chad settled on the firm leather sofa across from him, squirming to keep as much weight off his tender ass as possible. He looked up and caught Adam's gaze. "Look, I was thinking of a possible way to—"

"Not now. Now we need to have a serious discussion about your training. You'll need a safe word, a word you wouldn't normally use in conversation. Then if we're in the middle of a session and it becomes too intense for you, all you have to do is use that word and everything stops."

"It does?"

"Of course. We might come back to what we were doing at a later time, but safe words stop all play. I actually like to use two words, one to stop and one just to slow down. For example, 'red' and 'yellow,' like the stop and the caution lights. If you say 'yellow' then everything slows down or pauses while we discuss what's happening. Then we could either move on or decide you've had enough. It's all a negotiation, you see, a complete power exchange."

"I'm not following the power exchange thing. Seems to me the Dom has all the power."

Adam shook his head. "Not at all. Some people say the sub has all the power, but I think power is somewhat shared. A Dom directs what happens, but the sub directs what's allowed to happen. Everything a Dom does to a sub is consensual and negotiated ahead of time. It's a Dom's job to push the sub to his limits though. That's why subs have both hard and soft limits, but a sub can always stop everything immediately with just one word."

"Then what's the point?"

"The point is mutual pleasure, of course."

Shaking his head, Chad asked, "What do you mean by hard and soft limits?"

"A hard limit is something a sub or a Dom would never do, under any circumstances. Edge play, for example, or water sports. Soft limits are things that sound scary or distasteful to the either of the partners, but they might be willing to try them."

"I don't even know what the fuck those things are, but okay, I get what you mean."

Adam sighed. "Do you remember what I told you the first day we met in the restaurant?"

Chad nodded. His mind went back to those words that still echoed in his head. "Yes. Allowing another person to take away all of your control relieves you from making even the most basic decision. In return, that person give you more pleasure than you thought possible and lets you know you've been taken in hand, taken care of completely with no worries except how to please him and give him everything he wants. Everything he needs. Things only you can give him. In return, he'd take you to places you never even dreamed about."

A breathless silence in the room made Chad aware of his surroundings again. For just a few seconds, as Chad recited the things Adam told him that first day almost verbatim, Chad had gotten a little lost in his thoughts. He snapped his gaze back to Adam whose mouth was parted in surprise. "Uh, is that right?"

Adam nodded, his eyes dark and his voice low and silky. "Yes, that's right. Thank you for paying such close attention. I'd like to teach you about that if you'll let me. I think you should truly submit to me and feel what it's like. All you have to do is relax and leave everything to me."

As tense and wound up as he was, Chad said truthfully, "I don't think relaxing is possible."

"It is, if you'll put yourself in my hands."

Chad dropped his eyes. "I guess I could do that. No one will see me or anything, right? No one has to know about this?"

"If that's what you want. I think this is something you need for the case. Do you trust me, Chad?"

Chad looked up directly into Adam's eyes. "Yeah, I think I do. You helped me out last night, even if what happened embarrasses the hell out of me. I..ah...I'm glad if somebody had to do that—the spanking thing—I'm glad it was you."

"Why is that, Chad?"

"I-I don't know, really. I think I know you don't want to seriously hurt me."

Adam nodded. "I have no desire at all to hurt you. That's not really what I like, anyway. For me, it's more about control and domination, although I'm perfectly willing to indulge my sub in a bit of pain if he needs it."

"If he needs it? Why would anybody need pain?" Chad shook his head. "See this is the thing I'm not getting about BDSM. Why do some people seem to enjoy and want pain? And why do others seem to enjoy and want to inflict it?"

42

"Again, it's a complicated issue. I'm not a psychologist, and I don't pretend to be, but pain is all relative. It's really more about how rough you like it. Sadists, at least the ones I know, only want to give their willing partners what they need, what gets them excited. They'd have no interest in playing with someone who didn't want what they were giving them."

"What about the other guy? The masochist?"

"Again, there are as many different answers to that question as there are people. The easy answer is that it's something they give to their partner. They're giving them their pain and their submission to it willingly. It gets them both off to do that. It's exciting and edgy, and it demonstrates total submission to the other's needs."

"I still don't get it."

"Maybe because you're not a masochist, and that's okay. Different strokes, as they say. I would like to point out that last night when I had you across my lap, though, you had quite an erection. Do you know why?"

"I was clearly out of my head with the drug," Chad said, a little belligerence creeping back in his tone.

"You were drugged, yes, but I think you also enjoyed it. Maybe not the pain, but the humiliation and the control I had over you. The submission. If you were really my sub, we'd find out." Chad's gaze flicker up to his face. "I can see it embarrasses you, but as you said, it's just the two of us here. Nobody will ever know about our conversations, I can assure you. Nor will they ever know about anything we decide to do." He paused for effect before adding, "For practice."

Chad nodded, dropping his gaze.

"If you really were my sub, instead of just this role-play we're doing," Adam continued, his voice soft and almost hypnotizing in the quiet room, "I'd explore that with you more. It would be my job as your partner in this to help you explore it. I'd push your boundaries a little, to see how much you wanted. How much you needed it. Then if it was something we wanted to explore together, we could do some mild pain training."

"Pain training?" Chad could hear how thin and high his voice was getting, and he cleared his throat.

"A not-so-great term meaning how rough you wanted it. You might only want spankings. Spanking can be for fun sometimes too, as well as for punishments. It's about the intensity. You might also find you enjoy a flogger, which can cause more heat than pain, depending on how it's used. That kind of thing. Does any of that interest you?"

"Interest me? N-No, of course not. We're just talking, right?"

Adam smiled reassuringly. "We're just talking." He crossed his legs and regarded Chad solemnly for a long moment. "Can I ask you a question and not have you shouting back at me?"

Shrugging, he nodded. "Sure, I guess so."

"Have you ever been…curious about your sexuality?"

"No." He answered a bit too quickly, looked up, met Adam's eyes and saw nothing but kindness and interest. No censure or blame. He started to shake his head again, but found that he was nodding a little. "Okay, that's a lie. Maybe I have a little. I've never done anything about it, though, and never would."

"Why?"

"Why?" he echoed incredulously. "I'm a cop, that's why. God, if anybody I worked with even thought I was…my parents and my family would…they'd never…" He broke off, feeling his cheeks burning. "Just, no way."

Adam nodded. "You've told me what everybody else wants and expects from you. What about what you want? Doesn't that matter?" He smiled again. "No one is asking you to march in any gay pride parades or anything like that, but lying to yourself isn't exactly healthy either. You told me that first day we met that you didn't have a girlfriend. Why is that? You're a very attractive man."

Chad's gaze flew back up to his face, and Adam chuckled. "What? You don't like me saying I find you attractive? I do. I think you're one of the most attractive men I've ever met."

Surprised at how warm that made him feel, he smiled. "I-uh-I guess that's okay. Flattering… and to answer your question, I don't know why I don't have a girlfriend exactly. Of course, I've dated a lot, but I work a lot of strange hours, for one thing. It's hard to fit a steady relationship in, you know? Besides I haven't found anyone I really like, I guess."

"Because what you really like are men."

The statement wasn't loud or pushy or sarcastic. It was just a quiet affirmation, because it wasn't a question at all. Chad opened his mouth to say something and put him in his place, but then he looked into Adam's eyes. The expression in them was so calm, so accepting. No mockery. No judgment. Instead of the harsh answer that sprang to his lips, he swallowed hard and simply said, "Yeah, maybe."

Adam's gaze dropped. "Is that something you'd like to explore?"

Surprised, even a little shocked, Chad stood up restlessly and paced to the window, looking out to see if he could see any of the surveillance people around. Of course, he couldn't, if they were doing their jobs correctly, and he knew he was only buying time before he answered. He was hyper-aware of Adam waiting patiently for him to decide. Finally, he found his voice and turned to answer. "No. No, I can't."

Adam simply nodded. "All right." Was that a look of disappointment in Adam's eyes? If it was, it was gone too quickly for him to be sure. Adam stood up and stretched. "This is a great deal for you to take in at once. Take some time to think about it."

"Yeah, okay, so I might go home for a while. Check on my apartment and stuff. I'll probably be late. I can use my key to get back in later tonight. Maybe a break would help. See you in the morning."

"Afternoon more than likely. I leave quite early, and my first class starts at ten. I'll be on campus tomorrow until around three. You can work from here all morning, if you like. Or come and go as you please. It would help establish our cover. Then I'll see you when I get in around three o'clock."

"Okay, and…thanks for everything you did last night and for talking to me about…all of this."

The barest hint of a smile turned up the corners of his mouth. "My pleasure, Chad. See you tomorrow."

4

On the ride home to his apartment, Chad went over every word he and Adam had spoken to each other, as well as every glance, every nuance of expression. He slammed his hand down on the steering wheel. Why couldn't he admit he was attracted to the man? Adam had practically given him an engraved invitation, damn it, and still Chad lied and told him he wasn't interested in exploring the attraction and not just because of the kink aspect. Some of that actually intrigued him. Snatches of memory from the night before kept flickering through his brain as well. He didn't even want to think about what it meant that they were coming back more frequently as the day wore on, giving him a painful erection, not only with what had happened but how he'd thought and reacted while it was coming down.

He didn't want to think any more, either, that while admitting to someone else he was probably gay, he had admitted it to himself. The mere thought seeping into his head almost made him swerve off the road. Not gay, really. More like bi, though he hadn't been interested in a woman in far too long. At the moment it wasn't any woman he'd been with or knew springing to mind. All he could see in his head was a pair of warm, brown eyes staring back at him.

Everything about Adam Morrison was attractive to him, his eyes and the little bit of wave in his hair he probably tried to straighten with a hairdryer. Chad had noticed it though, at breakfast that morning. Even though he'd been upset and shouting, he still noticed every detail of Adam's appearance. Especially his body and the way his ass and his package filled those faded tight jeans.

Oh, God, I am so fucked.

Before he reached home his hands started shaking. He nearly ran inside, seeking refuge from his thoughts. They followed him, nagging at him as he checked everything methodically. Everything was fine. No longer than he'd been gone there was no reason for it not to be. He rummaged through the freezer for something to eat and found pizza rolls. He popped those in the microwave to heat and grabbed a can of cola. Plopped in front of the television to eat, he flipped through the channels. Finding a sci-fi channel, he settled down to watch, but after sitting through an entire movie, he had no idea what it was about, unable to concentrate.

The pizza rolls gave him indigestion, and he thought about what Adam would say if he knew what he'd had for lunch. The way Adam ate he probably wouldn't approve of frozen pizza rolls. At least Chad knew now what a fucking frittata was. Adam probably wouldn't approve of the cola either. All he ever drank with meals was water.

Fuck! Since when did Adam Morrison approving or disapproving of what he ate or drank matter? Where did the thought even come from?

He put his dish in the dishwasher and can in the recycling bin. Looking for something to do, he wandered restlessly back to the living room, craving something he couldn't put a name to. Why couldn't he admit to Adam he wanted to know what sex between two men would be like? Would that have made it too real? Thinking about men, browsing through websites kept it at a distance, easy to mark it off as simply curiosity, a sinful thrill, telling himself probably every man did the same thing. Not so easy looking into Adam's eyes or lying naked across his lap, his cock squeezed between strong thigh muscles—Fuck! An erection, immediate and big, had him shooting to his feet to adjust himself.

He stomped into the bathroom, stripping off his clothes, and got into the shower. Adjusting the temperature as cold as he could stand it, he stood there waiting for the damn hard-on to go down. It didn't. All he could think about was those rhythmic slaps on his ass, with his dick between Adam's strong thighs. Hand to his aching cock, he leaned his forehead against the tiles. Adam's voice in his head kept saying wicked, embarrassing things to him, like "Sweet boy, take the rest of your spanking…come for me, baby." With a groan, Chad shot off so hard he slumped against the wall and had to brace his feet to keep them from slipping out from under him.

Cold water beat down on him for five more minutes before he felt recovered enough to turn off the useless stream and climb out of the shower. Dried off and sitting on the side of the bed, he ran his hands through his damp hair. Maybe he needed to experiment with being gay. Really face it for once and find out the truth about himself. Maybe it was only a fantasy and wouldn't be anything he wanted if he actually experienced it. A hand job or a blow job wouldn't be so awful, would it? He could go to one of those bars and pick somebody up. See if they were interested in a one-off. Actually, it would take some of the tension off him with Adam.

Adam was helping with the investigation and anything to do with him outside of the job was totally inappropriate. Sure, what happened the night before had happened. Nothing he could do about it, except not repeat the mistake and not even think about how attractive he found the professor to be. No, he had to find some anonymous man and just explore this thing. Nobody had to know. No time like the present.

Not stalling a minute longer, he pulling out a pair of dark jeans and a T-shirt that had shrunk a little in the wash. Too tight, it really clung to his body like a second skin. He didn't put on any underwear, feeling bold and only a little embarrassed. Studying himself in the mirror, he thought he looked okay and ran his hands through his hair to smooth it down. Grabbing his car keys, he went out to his car before he could think about this thing too hard and talk himself out of it. He knew of a gay bar on the east side of town and headed his car in that direction. He was doing this, and now that it was actually going to happen, excitement built.

He reached the club in only a few minutes, and the parking lot was only half full. Determinedly, he got out of the car and went inside. The music was loud, and the room dark enough it took a second or two for his eyes to adjust. He went over to the bar and ordered a beer, with a shot chaser, adrenaline pumping through his veins.

His jeans got tight again at the idea of why he was there. Damn, he needed a drink and another orgasm bad. He downed three beers and more shots and pretty soon felt no pain at all. He was cruised hard by several guys as the evening wore on, but they didn't feel right to him. He turned them down. Into his fourth beer it dawned on him that the reason none of the men were right was because none of them were Adam.

Damn it. He slammed his mug down on the bar and a soft voice beside him said, "Be careful or you'll spill it. Beer's too expensive in this place to waste a drop."

He turned to find a tall young guy sitting beside him. Chad had been so lost in his thoughts he hadn't even noticed him slipping onto the stool beside him. He was probably a student, but looked to be old enough. He wondered how old he was and wasn't aware he'd said the words out loud until the boy next to him laughed and said, "I'm twenty-two. How old are you?"

"Old enough to know better," he said softly. He looked the young man up and down. He was about the right size, and his hair was almost the right color, that soft shade of brown. He angled his body toward him. The young man ran his hand up Chad's thigh, and Chad didn't pull away. He finished his shot and let his gaze roam over the guy, wondering just how to approach him for sex. Where would they go? Back to his car, maybe? He didn't have to worry for long.

The young man took his hand and pulled. "Let's go to the back room. I can give you what you need."

Without a word, Chad slipped off the stool and followed him to a dark room in the back. This guy was making the decisions for him, making everything easier, and already his cock was responding. With the other guy directing things, it took some of the pressure off him, right? Another couple had made it there before them, but that didn't seem to matter to his companion. He pushed Chad against the wall and slid to his knees, his hands busy at the zipper of Chad's jeans. He pulled him out and deep-throated him like a pro, and all Chad could do was grab onto his head and hold on for the ride. He threaded his fingers through the man's hair and leaned back against the wall, just letting the sensations of the guy's talented tongue and mouth take over everything.

This was definitely the way to go, an anonymous blow job with a talented tongue, no connections and no relationship to be made. Hell, he didn't even know the guy's name. He didn't have to worry about some man calling him his baby or his sweet boy or how humiliating words like that made him feel. He could go on with his life and get Adam out of his goddamned head. He looked down then as the man glanced up at him through a fringe of brown hair, his eyes dark green. Through a haze of alcohol, those green eyes registered in Chad's brain. No, they shouldn't be green eyes—that wasn't right. Those eyes should be brown. Realization swept over him. What the fuck was he doing? It was only Adam he wanted.

He put a hand down on the young man's head and gently pushed him away. The guy fell back on his heels with a puzzled look, his lips red and wet. "I-I'm sorry," Chad said, shaking his head. Side-stepping away, tucking himself back in his pants, he mumbled more to himself than the boy. "I'm sorry, but I-I can't."

He stumbled back through the bar and almost ran to his car, his cheeks burning with shame. He shouldn't be here. He had to get away. Starting his car, he turned out of the parking lot, not toward home, but toward Adam's house. He needed to talk to him, to try to figure this out. He knew Adam would know what to say to make him feel better. Still coherent enough to know he'd had way too much to drink to be driving, he slowed down and concentrated on making it to Adam's neighborhood and breathed a sigh of relief when he pulled into the driveway. Damn, he was dizzy, and he felt like shit. He was too fucking drunk to talk anyway. Maybe it would be best to go straight to his room to sleep it off. He was at the point where he didn't even trust himself to get into the house without letting the surveillance team see how drunk he was.

Getting from his car to the door, he did okay, or thought he did anyway. Over confident, he didn't turn on a light, stumbled over a rug in the entry hallway and almost fell. Managing to catch himself, he slammed into a small table by the wall. He grabbed for it and righted it, but something sitting on top flipped over his arm and crashed to the floor before he could catch it. Cursing, he squatted down and felt around with his fingertips, trying to pick up the pieces. Please God, don't let it be some priceless antique. He found a shard of glass by jamming it into his thumb and exclaimed before he could stop himself. Sticking this thumb in his mouth instinctively, he was still squatting on the floor when the lights came on.

Adam stood in the hallway wearing only soft looking pajama bottoms, not saying a word, his eyes taking in the scene in front of him. Chad fell on his butt, no longer with enough balance to maintain the squat, and pulled his thumb from his mouth. "I fell."

"I can see you did," Adam said softly, a hint of amusement in his voice. "And you broke my lamp, and now you're bleeding on my rug."

"I am?" He jammed his thumb back in his mouth, not knowing what else to do with it and looked around helplessly.

Adam made a noise in the back of his throat and hauled him to his feet. "Is this going to be a habit with you, Chad? Because if it is, the county needs to think about putting me on its payroll and giving me extra hazard pay."

"I-I'm sorry," he said, stumbling along behind Adam as he pulled him down the hall. "I didn't mean to wake you."

"Mm-hmm, well, you did. How much have you had to drink tonight anyway?" He took Chad into the guest room and deposited him on the side of the bed.

"Just a few beers and some shots."

"A few, huh? Did a cab bring you then?" He crossed to the window and looked out at Chad's car in the driveway before turning back to him, furious. "No, I can see you drove here, you complete idiot. It's not enough for you to try to kill yourself, you have to drag innocent bystanders into the deal."

He'd reached the stage he usually devolved to whenever he had too much to drink. "I'm sorry, okay? I fucked up." He lowered his head back to his hands and groaned. "Damn it, I feel like I'm about to fly apart!" He jumped to his feet and looked around for something to punch. When he couldn't find anything to take out his anger on, he drove his fist into the wall. "Damn it!"

"Stop that right now." Adam's voice wasn't loud, but it was firm and conveyed a kind of take no prisoners tone. "Sit down on the bed and show me your hand."

Chad turned and almost missed the bed, but managed to fall down onto it and right himself. He held up the offending appendage for Adam to see, feeling sullen and unable to make eye contact with him. Adam took his hand firmly in his and pressed his fingers gently into it, causing Chad to

50

wince. "Nothing broken, no thanks to you."

He pulled Chad's T-shirt over his head and wrapped it around his hand. "This will stop the bleeding at least. Sit still while I get some bandages." He turned at the door and pointed a finger. "Don't you dare move."

Sunk in misery, Chad sagged on the bed, but jumped when Adam returned almost at once with a small first aid kit. Adam sat down beside him and in a business-like manner cleaned and swabbed out his wound and none too gently, either. There were still some pieces of glass in the cut, but he picked them out, and pressed antiseptic to the cut with a cloth. "No stitches, I think, but it's a nasty cut. I'm going to put some antibiotic cream on it and bandage it for you."

He did as he said, and in a few minutes, Chad's thumb was bandaged neatly. He started up, and Adam pushed him firmly back down. "You only move when I tell you to. Understand?"

Chad was capable of understanding the command even if his thought processes didn't advance enough to understand why he should follow it. He nodded, freezing in position.

"Take off your pants, go to the bathroom, and I'll be back in a minute."

Go to the bathroom? Come to think of it, he was rather desperate to pee. He rolled off the bed to his knees, pushed up, nearly going to his face on the floor when his hand slipped, and stumbled into the adjoining bathroom. Pulling out his dick, he remembered the last time it had been out. He closed his eyes and groaned. Was it possible to die of embarrassment? As much of it as he'd suffered through the past couple of days, it must not be. More's the pity.

He finished up and washed his hands, careful not to get his new bandage wet, a good excuse not to look at himself in the mirror before he stumbled back to the bedroom wanting nothing more than to lie down and die.

Adam waited for him, his mouth pressed in a tight line. "Pants off, Chad. Now."

He slipped them down, not even blushing over the fact he was commando. Not much, anyway. Swaying a little, he waited for whatever Adam had to say next. Instead of saying anything, Adam shoved him backward. Chad fell on his back on the bed. Adam took his wrist in one hand and a leather cuff appeared in the other. He slipped it on Chad's wrist, neatly attaching the other end to the bed post.

Adam looked at it stupidly. "What is that?"

"That's a cuff, Chad. And here's a matching one."

The second appeared in his hand. It took Chad that long to understand he was picking them up from the floor and what he was doing to him. Adam snapped the second one on, leaned over Chad, holding him down with a hand in his chest, and attached it to the opposite post. Chad's efforts to stop him were about effective as hammering a nail with a rolled up newspaper.

Chad pulled hard on the cuffs, but they weren't budging. Adam pulled more cuffs from the floor next to him and attached one to Chad's ankle and to the post on the footboard, Chad's drunken resistance useless. The other ankle got the same treatment. Chad pulled at his bonds experimentally. Nothing hurt or was too tight, but he couldn't move, for sure. He got a little angry.

"What the fuck do you think you're doing, Professor?"

"Giving you what you came here for tonight, Chad. Think of this as a time-out. You can't seem to control your actions, so I'm doing it for you. Lie there, contemplate your sins, and sleep it off."

* * * *

Adam hadn't been so turned on in a long time. He stared down at Chad, naked and wearing nothing but his cuffs with his angry red prick pointed toward the ceiling. Adam was having a hard time convincing himself it would be wrong to uncuff Chad's legs, throw them over his shoulders and fuck him into the mattress.

"Since you came in drunk with your zipper down and wearing no underwear, I'd say you've been out to experiment. Is that right?"

Chad nodded.

"And how far did you get?"

"To the back room of a bar with a guy who was giving me a blow job," he slurred miserably.

Adam dropped his gaze, surprised at the fierce anger and outrage racing through him. This was his boy, damn it. "I see."

"I didn't...I mean, he didn't finish. I wouldn't let him. I-I pushed him away and ran out of there."

"Why did you do that, Chad?"

"Because...because he wasn't...he wasn't ..." He let his head fall back against the pillows.

The last words were almost whispered, and Adam sat down beside him to lean closer. "He wasn't what?" He allowed himself to trail a finger down Chad's sculpted chest and down to his abs. Dipping the finger into his bellybutton, he watched as Chad squirmed. Ticklish. Good to know.

He waited for the longest time, until he thought he wasn't going to get a reply at all. Then the words came so softly he almost missed them. "You...he wasn't you, and I couldn't stop thinking about how it should have been."

Adam had to press his lips together hard to keep from smiling. He needed to stay stern and in control, but he badly wanted to hug his boy and give him a good spanking for even thinking about allowing someone else to touch him. This was the second time in as many days someone else had their hands and mouths all over his boy, and that shit was going to stop.

"Thinking of me, huh? With your dick stuck down somebody else's throat?"

"I…I'm sorry, Adam."

"Don't do it again. If you're very good and you can convince me you're very sorry, I may let you go in the morning."

"But-but you can't just leave me here like this," he complained, bouncing his hips in an unconsciously suggestive invitation.

Though it was difficult, he ignored the seductive, jiggling cock. "Oh, I could and I should. But since you've decided to practically give yourself alcohol poisoning, I won't, in case you might vomit and choke to death. It would be just like you. So I'll be over there." He pointed to a chaise lounge by the window. "Probably spending a very uncomfortable night. I wish you the same."

"But wait—I th-think I want you to m-make love to me."

"And I think that's the alcohol talking. No, hush now. When you're sober and make that statement, we'll discuss it again."

Adam grabbed a pillow and a blanket off the bed, ignoring Chad's whimper, stomped over to the chaise, and tried to make himself comfortable. Without a doubt he wouldn't be. His cock strained against even the looseness of his pajama bottoms. He wanted so badly to sink it in Chad's sweet little ass.

He got very little sleep, waking up several times to check on Chad when he murmured or groaned in his sleep. Once he sat by him for a few minutes on the side of the bed, just gazing down at him. Chad's mouth was open, and soft, wet snores came from his throat. He tried to roll over on his stomach and when he couldn't, he'd got a frown on his handsome face and puffed out his lips like a pouty three year old. Adam thought he was exquisite in his struggles.

Smiling, he went back over to the uncomfortable chaise and planned how he would handle Chad in the morning. Once he'd figured it out, he smiled and settled down to try to get some sleep before he had to get up.

At seven o'clock, when the alarm went off in the master down the hall, Adam got up and showered. He wandered into the kitchen for a cup of coffee, grateful for the timer he always set the night before on the coffee maker. He ate some fruit and small bowl of cereal and was almost ready to leave.

With a small smile playing around his lips, he went to his room and got what he needed, then walked back into Chad's room. He was still softly snoring. Pulling back the covers, he admired the sight before him. Chad had some morning wood. That would make this even sweeter. He reached beneath him and gave his ass a hard pinch, hard enough to wake Chad right up.

He cried out and came awake sputtering, coughing, and trying to pull his hand down to rub his ass. "What? What the hell?"

Adam looked down at him. Chad's erection had flagged because of the pain and shock of being pinched, and his pretty cock lay curled up defenselessly on his thigh. Adam quickly picked it up, put it into the cock cage, and turned the key in the lock.

Chad looked down at himself incredulously. "W-What are you doing?" he yelled.

"Putting you in a cock cage. I believe the punishment should fit the crime, don't you? You shared yourself with some stranger last night without permission. This cock belongs to me now, Chad, until we end our training. It's now under my supervision."

"You can't do that!" Chad struggled against his cuffs and cursed loudly. "Damn it, let me out of these cuffs and get that damn thing off of me."

Adam crossed his arms over his chest. "No. We're practicing, remember? Drinking and putting yourself yet again in a dangerous situation with driving in that condition is not to be tolerated. Since we're not in a true relationship, and I understand how confused you are, I'll partially excuse your infidelity—this time. Normally, your punishment for allowing another man to even touch you would have been much more severe if not a reason to kick you out."

"And if I refused to submit to it, you'd call the relationship off?"

"Exactly. Since I'm about to leave, I'll consider—if you can change that attitude and ask me nicely—removing the cuffs now and the cage when I return home this afternoon."

The look on Chad's face was priceless, and the struggle going on inside his head must have been epic. Adam enjoyed watching it a great deal. After a great deal of grimacing and huffing and puffing, Chad managed to speak.

"Would you please let me out of these cuffs? Sir."

Adam pretended to consider it a moment before nodded. Using one of the keys on his key ring, he loosened first his ankles and then his wrists. Chad sat up and pulled at the cage.

"Ow!" he yelled.

"Well, for God's sake, Chad, if you pull at it like that, of course it's going to hurt. I can assure you it's not coming off without the key." He stuck his keys in his pocket and took a step back as Chad lunged off the bed, looking like he was coming after him.

"Don't you dare," he said sternly. Chad stopped immediately and even looked horrified at his own actions. Good. His boy was learning. "You know what happened last night was wrong. Out of control. If you refuse to take the punishment you deserve, and want to use your safe word, now's the time."

Chad opened and closed his mouth several times before finally crossing his arms over his chest with that adorable pout again.

"All right. You have my number if you decide to use your safe word. I can be home reasonably soon if you call."

"If I can't stand it anymore and call you? What then?"

"The cage is designed for long-term use, so it shouldn't be all that uncomfortable unless you pull at it. If you try to get it off on your own and don't take your punishment, I'll call the chief to end this whole thing. I'll give him the key, and he can be the one to let you out."

At the look of horror on Chad's face, Adam almost smiled, but that would be cruel, and he really wanted Chad to learn from this experience. He had no intention of calling the chief, but it wouldn't hurt to make him think he might.

Adam turned to go, but he was stopped at the door by Chad's plea. "But I-I have to pee," he said, his face a bright red.

"Go ahead. The cage doesn't prevent you from that. Only from getting an erection." He turned to leave again and called over his shoulder. "Be a good boy." He glanced back at him. "Don't worry. Your pants will fit over it."

"You expect me to go to work like this?" Chad's voice was low and tight with anger.

"Why not? Have a nice day, Pet, and I expect I'll see you when I get home." Listening to Chad's muffled curse, he smiled and left for the gym.

* * * *

With a mother of all hangovers on top of world class humiliation, Chad gave serious consideration to not going in to work at all, but damn it, he had a job to do. Nothing could free his cock from that cage without inflicting painful injury. He searched through his clothes for the loosest pair of pants he'd brought along even though the cage didn't show at all, even through his underwear. He just wanted to avoid any stimulation of even his pants rubbing against his cock. Meeting the dress code for the day was the least of his worries.

He'd fucking done it again and made a king-sized ass of himself in front of Adam again. If his memories were anywhere near accurate, he'd also told the bastard he wanted him to make love to him only to be turned down. Okay, maybe Adam was only not taking advantage of his drunken state, like he said, and yeah, maybe Chad would never have had the guts to said it if he hadn't been drunk. He'd probably never have gone into that backroom with a stranger either. Was it bottled courage or did drink deaden inhibitions based on lifetime prejudices?

Right now, he was sober, madder than hell at Adam for the embarrassing cock cage, and still wanted him like he'd never wanted anybody before. The result was more than discomfort. The cage was actually a misnomer in that it wasn't a big bulky box that fit over his groin, as the name implied. This one, at least, was simply a device that fit snugly over his penis and locked at the base of his shaft, so that every time he tried to get an erection, he swelled up against the restricting bars which hurt like a bitch and killed his erection. Of course, he was very aware of the device and why he was wearing it as well as who was making him wear it, and his cock constantly tried to get a hard-on.

All in all, it didn't put him in a very good mood. He barely sat down at his desk to catch up on paper work when the captain called him to his office. Fighting the urge to adjust his cage and hoping he wasn't walking funny with how strange it felt, he braced himself for censure, certain his condition the night before had been noticed and reported.

"How did the weekend go?"

"Okay."

"Okay?"

"Made a showing at the funeral and the club and met some of the others who received letters. He's got a thing planned to introduce me to some more of them this week, after he gives me some more training."

"And how is that going?"

"I'm going to survive it," he said, clipping his words off more than he meant to. Catching himself, he admitted, "It could have been better when we went to the club. I screwed up, embarrassed him in front of his friends, and he sent me away. He covered my blunder telling them I'm in training."

"You're having trouble with it?" he asked, looking like he was braced for an explosion.

"I don't get the concept, at least not entirely. I am learning how to behave the way he wants me to. He's got me practicing while we're alone so I can perform properly when we're out." God he hoped he wasn't blushing. He did squirm before he could stop himself. At least he didn't reach for his caged cock. In self-defense, he changed the subject. "I haven't had a chance to ask Philips or Johansson yet if they've found any connection to Jeremy Rubin and any of the hate groups?"

"We're getting search warrants to force them to turn over their member lists. None of them will willingly talk to us, and if they knew we were onto someone specific, they'd warn the bastard. None of the confidential informers recognize the name, either."

"None of them are responsible for the letters?"

"If they are, the general membership doesn't know about it. Everything indicates he's doing this on his own." He drew a deep breath and added, "If it's him."

"He looks good for it to me."

"It's the best lead we've gotten so far, but still the only real connection to the University is that some of the professors and students attend his brother's church. We haven't been able to locate any work history, meaning he's either never worked a steady job or has worked all of his life taking his wages in cash under the table. No bank accounts, either, at least not locally. If he has a cell phone, we can't find any record of it."

"Sounds like you're going ahead with a deep search."

"Because I'm desperate. We're just being damned careful not to tip him off."

"Eyes on him yet?"

"Yeah, I put a team in place. They caught up with him leaving the house last night, after dark so no decent photos. He headed toward the Atlanta highway, and they lost him. Did Morrison mention the fact the brothers fight like cats and dogs?"

"No, but I'm not surprised from the conversation I overheard. Jason talked about reforming him. Adam did say Jeremy is unpleasant. He also said they look enough alike that he at first mistook Jeremy for Jason. Are they sure they had the right guy?"

"No doubt. They preacher came home, all spit and polish. They yelled at each other for half an hour, the scum came out, hair spiked, jeans hanging off his ass with holes in the knees. He shouted back that he was taking his car and hoped to hell he was asleep when he got back. Laid rubber going out in his brother's car, too. Sounds like your professor was being nice when he called him unpleasant."

"What were they arguing about?"

"They weren't close enough to understand the words."

"Where did he go?"

His boss grunted. "Good question. After they lost him, they set up back at his house. He didn't go back until nearly dawn. We don't have any idea where he went or what he did."

Chad shot to his feet. "How the hell did he ditch them? He knew he was being followed?"

"No, it wasn't anything like that. Calm down. A truck pulled out between them. Before they could get around it, he'd disappeared."

"There weren't any murders last night."

"No, but he could be stalking his next target." He flopped back in his chair. "I know this is hard for you, but if you think of anything to bring more attention to you, let me know. Right now that's the only hope we have."

"You've got people on any others who might have received letters, don't you?"

"Those we know about. Not everyone is as open as your professor."

Spinning for the door, Chad retorted, "I'm going through all the notes in the files, every fucking interview, and see if I can find something they missed. As he walked out he added, "And he's not my professor." He was pretty happy about making that clear, until he walked away and some pubic hair got caught in the cage so he had to adjust himself. Shit, more like the other way around.

* * * *

With the last class over, Adam walked out of Park Hall and looked up at the sky. It was a beautiful day, if a little chilly. Rather than go immediately to his car, he took the campus bus to the downtown area and strolled across the street to do a little shopping for Chad. A small specialty boutique he went to from time to time carried some of the things he had in mind. After leaving, he stopped by a men's store to buy some jeans and slacks in Chad's size, along with a few shirts a bit dressier than the T-shirts that seemed to make up a large portion of his off-duty wardrobe. He walked back to the bus stop and rode the campus bus to his car. Glancing at his watch, he saw that it was almost five o'clock. Chad had been in the cock cage for over ten hours and would probably be beside himself by now. Not that the device was all that uncomfortable. He'd had some of his subs wear them for days, but this was the first time for Chad, so he knew Chad would be more than ready to get the device off when he got home.

Sure enough, when he pulled into the garage, the door to the kitchen opened up right away, and Chad stood framed in the doorway.

"Where have you been? You said you'd be home by three, damn it."

Adam got out of the car. Allowing himself only one look to let Chad know how he felt about his attitude, he took his time getting his packages and briefcase. Chad was smart and probably a little desperate.

He lowered his gaze immediately, shoving his hands in his pocket. "I-I'm sorry. I was worried."

Remembering why Chad was here in the first place, Adam stopped short. "Oh shit, I'm sorry. It never even occurred to me you'd be worried." It was true. Ever since Chad crashed into the house the night before, he'd been so consumed with thoughts of him that the murder investigation had taken a back seat. He needed to get his head back on straight. "From now on, I'll stick firmly to my schedule. All right?"

"The people working surveillance should have had you all day, so it was probably okay. They're supposed to be following you. I'll call tonight and make sure."

"Okay." Adam set his bags down on the floor near the kitchen table. "I'm hungry. I don't usually eat it, but shall I order some pizza for us tonight? Only because I'm too tired to cook. What kind do you like?"

Chad shook his head. "It doesn't matter, but-but what about this? Could you please, please get it off me? It's been bothering me all day." He gestured down toward his groin.

Adam took his time answering. He called and ordered dinner, a large vegetarian pizza, and then leaned back against the countertop. "Since you asked me nicely, and since this is your first time to wear one, I'll take it off after you tell me what you learned."

"That it's damned uncomfortable, and I never want to wear one again. Ever!"

Adam smiled. "What else?"

He wrinkled his brow and worried at his bottom lip with his teeth, obviously wanting to give the right answer, but coming up blank. Adam sighed. "Okay, who's in charge of your cock from now until this is over?"

"Oh." His cheeks turned a deep pink. "You are."

"It belongs only to me until this is over. You don't touch it either. Not without permission. That means no more jerking yourself off. Understand?"

His eyebrows rose. "Well, what's the point of that?"

"The point, Chad, is for you to learn obedience. This is one of the techniques I'm using. Once you learn to be obedient and look to me for everything, and I do mean everything, then the faster you'll be able to appear at the club or in front of my friends in a believable way. It's what you want, correct?"

"Yeah, I guess."

"Okay, drop your pants."

Adam didn't think it was possible for Chad's cheeks to get pinker, but they did, as he eased his jeans down past the cage and pushed them to his knees. Adam pulled out his keys, fit one of them in the lock and pulled the cage off. Chad sagged in relief until Adam pushed it back into his hand. "Go clean it with soap and hot water. Dry it off carefully and put in on my dresser."

"Okay," he said softly. He pulled his jeans back up and headed to the bathroom.

Adam laughed softly and went over to sit on the sofa in the den area. So he didn't like the cock cage. Something to remember for next time, because he had no doubt Chad would screw up again. As a matter of fact, he thought Chad might screw up on purpose, just to get a punishment. He'd said it was uncomfortable, and since the cage was designed for long-term wear, there was only one reason for that. His prick must have been trying to get hard all day long, and the cage prevented it.

He heard footsteps coming back down the hall and looked up with a smile when he saw Chad hovering near the door. "Come in, Chad, and sit down. Why are you standing there?"

"I didn't know. I—I mean you said you'd be training me now, and I didn't know if I was supposed to."

"Chad, this isn't a master-slave relationship, or, I mean, we're not pretending it is. I made you sit at my feet in the club and fed you because we were playing that night. At home, I might be in charge. I may even ask you to wear fewer clothes, but that's about it, unless you're being punished. I think I told you one time my subs in the past usually went without clothing at home."

"Um, yeah. I don't know if I can do that."

"Bring me the bags there by the table, will you?"

Chad brought them over and sat down on the sofa when Adam gestured for him to. Adam dug in the smallest bag and came out with a specially designed jock strap, the likes of which Chad had probably never seen before. Made of a pale blue thin, lightweight material, it was formed to create a pouch in front.

Chad asked, "Just what is this supposed to be?"

"A jock strap."

Chad scoffed. "This doesn't look like the old ones I used to keep in my gym bag in high school."

"No, it's nothing like the dirty, stretched out ones you no doubt wore in gym class."

Adam tossed it into Chad's lap. Chad poked at it with one finger. "It's not made like any I've ever seen either."

"That's for your package. It lifts you up and makes you look bigger. Not that you have any problems in that area, but it will enhance what you have and make you look good. I bought three of them, in different colors. This is what you'll wear at home instead of your usual underwear. Leave your shirt off too. That way, if one of my friends stops over, you can take off your jeans and just wear this, and they won't be suspicious."

Chad's face got red again, but he nodded. "Okay, I guess I can do that."

He swallowed hard and sighed, showing his resignation. Satisfied, Adam moved to the kitchen sink and washed his hands, not looking at Chad. "Why don't you put it on now and wear it around to get used to it?"

Only silence answered him while Adam rinsed the soap from his hands and dried them on a paper towel. Just when he decided Chad wasn't going to answer, Chad cleared his throat and said softly, "Yeah, I guess I could do that, too."

Adam nodded, still not looking at him, and Chad left the room. Damn, he was getting too involved with this man, after he promised himself he wouldn't. Leaving aside the kink aspect of the situation, Chad was in a profession known to be homophobic, had parents and family he worried about, and hadn't even been able to completely admit, even to himself, that he was gay. Adam had no business even thinking about an involvement with him. Any relationship with him would be too complicated. He liked his private life to be orderly and controlled. Life with Chad would be anything but. No, he had to pull back, and he would, starting now. Turning toward a slight noise behind him, his mouth went dry, and his mind corrected the thought. Starting tomorrow.

Chad stood in the doorway, his beautiful body wearing only the blue jock strap to match those icy blue eyes. He pivoted slowly and looked back over his shoulder. "I-uh-I'm pretty exposed here." Blue straps joined the waistband with an elegant arc of spandex, nicely displaying his butt cheeks. "Think I could have something a little more traditional?"

"You're not playing high school football, Chad. The idea is not to look like you just came in from the practice field, but to display your body. I think it looks very nice."

He turned back around. "Okay. Maybe I should wear it around a little—just to get the feel of it."

"Yes, I think that's a good idea."

The doorbell rang, and Chad whirled, a deer-in-the-headlights look on his face.

"Calm down, it's probably just the pizza guy. Go back in the bedroom so he can't see you, if you like."

Chad took off like a shot. Adam went to the door and paid for the pizza, then brought the box back down the hall, headed toward the kitchen. Chad poked his head out from the bedroom, saw the coast was clear, and followed Adam. Adam pulled out dishes and bottles of water, and they both perched on stools at the granite topped island to eat.

Afterward, Chad volunteered to clean up, saying, with a cute little smile, "I'll clean, since you cooked."

Adam tried not to stare at Chad's ass as he disposed of the box in the garbage and rinsed the dishes before putting them in the dishwasher, but it was a losing battle. He found himself sneaking peeks at the muscular behind every chance he got.

To distract himself, he picked up his briefcase and sat down in his chair. Turning on the television, he found a news program, before opening his briefcase and pulling out papers he needed to grade, the bane of a literature professor's existence. He often spent evenings like this, finding the monotony of it soothing, and it helped him to wind down after a stressful day. Tonight though, he was too aware of Chad sitting down a bit gingerly on the sofa, pulling at the strap and restlessly jiggling his leg. Adam waited him out. Before twenty minutes passed, Chad turned off the television.

"Nothing on."

Adam nodded.

Chad bounced his legs until Adam couldn't take it anymore. "Must you do that, Chad?"

Chad looked down at his knees. "Huh? Oh, sorry. I don't get why I'm so nervous. I just…I don't feel right. Something's wrong with me, and it's bothering me." He looked up with a pleading gaze that hit Adam hard.

Adam wanted badly to help him, and he thought he knew how. "I think I know what it might be. You're a strong man, Chad, and a responsible one," Adam said. "You want to take care of all the bad guys out there, but outside of work, I think you want to lay that burden down. You want someone else to take care of the details and take the load off your shoulders. In return, you want to take care of just one person. Be everything to that person and concentrate on doing whatever you can to make them happy. I don't think you even knew what it was you wanted until we talked in the restaurant. I saw the light in your eyes that day, but you're still afraid of it. Your reaction to your spanking convinced me further, but you still need me to spell it out for you, because you're scared to admit that what you are is a submissive, who you are is gay, and there's not a damn thing wrong with either one of those things."

"I…uh…" He cleared his throat and crossed his arms again, but his cock had begun to swell and was showing off quite nicely in his new jock strap.

Pointedly ignoring what Adam said and changing the subject, Chad asked, "So…uh, is this what you'd normally do in the evenings when you were with a boyfriend?"

"We weren't having orgies every night, if that's what you were thinking."

"Yeah, but don't you guys have like dungeon rooms where you take your subs? I mean, that's what it says in the books I've read."

He put down the paper he was reading and cocked his head. "What books you read? I sent you a list, but you said you never got around to reading any of them."

"Oh. Yeah. Not those. I mean like that Fifty Shades book. I might have skimmed through that one a little. Maybe a couple others, just to get a feel for it, you know."

"I see. No, I don't have a dungeon room. I go to the club for that kind of thing. I have some toys in a chest in my room, but as I told you, I'm not big into pain."

"Yeah, but you've done it, right? You've probably used the whips and stuff."

"I have, yes. Are you interested in that stuff?"

"Just curious. Like the other night in the club, when your friend said he was going to do a scene with his sub? Were they going to like have sex right there in front of everybody?"

"Not necessarily. Usually, a Dom will display his sub's obedience and submission. They could have done some CBT, or he could have used the spanking bench or a flogger. I got, um, distracted and didn't pay attention."

Chad shook his head. "Yeah, right. I remember what distracted you. But, uh, CBT? What is that?"

Adam smiled. "Cock and ball torture."

Chad straightened up on the couch. "No shit? Torture? Sounds awful."

"Not if you like to do it, and a lot of subs and Doms do."

"What does it consist of?"

Still smiling, Adam put down his papers and settled back in his chair. "A lot of different things. Clamps and weights attached to the balls. Sounding…even needles. Slapping and rough treatment of the cock and the scrotum, maybe. A cock ring so you can't come no matter how badly you might want to—there are several different methods."

"What the hell is sounding and what do you mean, needles?"

"Piercings," he said calmly. "And sounding is using a set of very thin surgical steel rods in graduating sizes, very thin to about the thickness of your little finger. They're inserted into the sub's penis into the uretha. Also known as cock stuffing."

"Jesus. I don't think I even want to know anymore. I don't think I could do anything like that."

"What would you like to try?" Adam was aware that the tone of his voice had gotten deeper and silkier. Chad in his current state of undress turned him on. The conversation was definitely adding to his arousal.

"Me? I-I don't necessarily want to try any of it."

"Necessarily?"

"You know what I mean. It's just that last night, when you cuffed me to that bed…"

"Yes? Go on," he coaxed when Chad's voice trailed off.

Chad dropped his gaze, and his face flushed. "It helped. I felt like I was about to come apart. That's why I slammed my fist in the wall and probably why I got so drunk in the first place. Tied down like that felt safe, in a way. I didn't have any choice but to lie still. All of this is getting to me, I guess. What you said a minute ago…about me being gay? I went to that bar to see, you know. I wanted to see if I was…well, if I was more than just curious, like we talked about yesterday."

"Did you find out?"

Chad turned back toward Adam and caught his gaze with his own. "I think I did. The guy I hooked up with sort of took charge and led me to the back room. I was scared, but interested, all right. It was easier for me to just follow his lead so I went to the backroom with him, but in the end, I couldn't go through with it."

"You couldn't?"

"No. I got scared and ran out of there. Fucking ran, like a kid or something. Then when I got here and you cuffed me…I tried to get out of them, you know, but I couldn't. There wasn't a thing I could do about any of it, except trust you to take care of me. It...relaxed me, somehow."

Adam nodded. "Because you're submissive."

Chad looked up sharply. "I don't know about that."

"Don't be so scared of it. It's just a word. I've tried to explain to you that submissives have all the power. They're strong people. It doesn't mean anything negative."

Chad squirmed a little on the couch. "Maybe so. I mean, I believe you, but it's still hard for me to talk about this. Hard for me, period."

"I know."

"No, you don't understand. What I'm trying to tell you is that last night I couldn't go through with it because I kept seeing...your face. It's not just that I think I might be—I could be gay, or even you know, submissive, or whatever. It's that I think...I think I want you."

Adam blinked. Well, that was direct. Ball in your court, professor. What are you going to do about it?

He took a deep breath. "Get up off that couch and go to my bedroom. Take that off, lie down on the bed, and wait for me." For one breathless moment, he thought Chad was going to balk in panic and refuse. He released the air out of his lungs softly when Chad slowly stood up and moved down the hallway, his bare feet making soft little padding sounds as he walked past his own room.

Adam took a deep breath, slowing himself down before he followed him. He watched from the doorway as Chad slipped the jock strap off and dropped it on the floor beside the bed. Naked as the day he was born, he stretched out on his back and stared straight into Adam's eyes.

Adam walked farther into the room, unbuttoning his shirt as he went and relishing Chad's steady gaze on him. He made his movements slow and deliberate, watching with satisfaction as Chad's cock grew thick and long, pointing upward. Adam pushed his underwear and trousers off in one smooth movement and stepped toward the bed, letting Chad's hungry gaze roam over his body.

"Are you sure you want this, Chad?"

He licked his lips. "I don't know what the hell I'm doing, but yeah, I want this. If it's you. If you'll show me what to do."

Adam smiled. "I'd be glad to show you."

5

Chad had thought about doing making love to Adam, rationalized it, analyzed it, and finally gave in to the idea. Drunk or sober, he wanted Adam. Adam's silky voice wrapped around Chad like a hug, making him feel warm and safe. He could look at Adam for hours and not get his fill. He was so damn beautiful, his body lean and graceful, his dick something to see. Longer than Chad's, though not so thick, it flared at the glans, and the shaft rose up from a thatch of trimmed dark hair. He stopped by the bed and let Chad look as much as he wanted.

Chad, nervous as hell, lowered his eyes, when Adam sat down on the bed beside him and rubbed his hand over Chad's chest, Adam's heat seeping into his bones.

"If you want to stop anything, tell me, and we will."

Chad nodded and for the first time in his life, he reached for another man's cock, wrapping his hand around it. The skin was satin smooth, with hard steel underneath, just like his own. Adam bent to kiss him, his hands on Chad's hips, just touching him, not holding him down. The kiss was the merest brushing of his lips against Chad's, but Chad's dick swelled even more. The mere desire to kiss another man almost made him lose control. Not just any man made him feel this way, but there was no denying Adam did.

Chad flicked at his lips with his tongue, just like he had with the girls he'd dated in the past. Adam parted his lips and let him in, but this was no girl he was kissing. Adam's cheeks, though smooth-shaven, were rougher against his skin, and his hands were big and strong on his hips. Adam sighed as Chad swept his tongue over the inside of his mouth and relaxed, letting his chest settle down onto Chad's, the hard muscles again reminding Chad he was not with a woman.

Chad pulled at him, urging him forward, and he came willingly, twisting

65

to climb on the bed without breaking the kiss and leaning partly on top of him. He threw one warm leg over Chad's, and a hard rod of flesh scorched Chad's hip.

Chad rocked his hips up against that heat and wasn't chided for moving too fast, like his last girlfriend used to do, telling him she needed more foreplay. Instead, Adam thrust back, and hooked an arm over Chad, his hand under Chad's ass to massage and squeeze.

Breaking the kiss, Chad looked up and him, grinned, and received a grin right back. Adam slid over on top of him and rubbed the length of his satin smooth cock over Chad's. With new, exhilarating sensations racing through him, Chad gasped and exclaimed softly, "Fuck."

Adam smiled and rubbed harder. "All in good time, baby." He released Chad's ass and turned his attention to his chest, circling his nipples with his fingers, pinching and pulling them and watching Chad's face.

"Oh, damn. That feels so…I don't know if I…"

Adam took one of his nipples in his mouth, moving his tongue and teeth over it gently.

"Shit!" Chad arched up, thrusting his groin hard into Adam's. Why had no one ever told him about his nipples being so sensitive? Again Adam thrust back. He caught Chad's mouth and slipped his tongue inside. Chad knew he wasn't going to last, and it embarrassed him to be so needy. He pulled his mouth away desperately. "I-I don't think I can last much longer."

"You won't come yet, baby. I don't want you to."

Chad ground his hard-on into him and moaned softly. Adam put a thumb and forefinger around the base of his cock and squeezed, harder than actually felt good. Chad jerked, his hand going to push Adam's away, but the urgent need to come receded a little into something more manageable.

"O-Okay," he said, breathing hard.

Adam removed his hand and stretched out over him again, slowed the thrusting down and rubbed his cock gently against Chad's. Dropping another kiss on his lips, he took Chad's wrists in his hands and stretched his arms up over his head, holding him there. He whispered against his lips.

"What do you want, baby?"

"I-I want you to fuck me."

He gazed down at Chad and one eyebrow quirked up. "Are you sure about this?"

"Yes. No. Oh shit, I don't know. Yes, I am. I want you to."

He kissed Chad gently again. "We don't have to, sweet boy. We can wait if you're not sure."

"No, no, I'm sure. With you…only you."

Adam sighed and shook his head. "Damn, the things you say to me." He nibbled at Chad's earlobe, making him squirm restlessly under him.

"Please," Chad whispered. "Please."

Before Chad had a chance to change his mind, Adam kissed him until he was breathless and his mind stopped going around in circles. Adam sat up on the side of the bed and pulled open the drawer in the bedside table for condoms and lube. He smoothed the condom on expertly and slicked it with lube. Turning back to the bed, he smiled at Chad and leaned over to kiss his stomach. "On your knees or face to face? It might hurt less with you on your knees."

"No, I want to see you, and I like the kissing."

"Mm, I like it too." He bent over for another slow kiss, and Chad pulled at his biceps, trying to hurry him along.

"There's no rush, sweetheart," Adam said against his lips. "Just relax and let me handle everything."

Adam hooked his hands under Chad's knees and pushed them toward his shoulders. "Hold your legs up, baby."

Doing as ordered, Chad caught a hold of his knees with his hands to hold them close to his chest. He looked Adam in the eye, trying to breathe normally while one finger slowly, gently, rubbed lube along his crease, stopping to tap against his hole. Holding air in his lungs, he tensed, waiting, but relaxed as nothing more happened than the gentle tapping and massaging at his rim. Jesus, did it feel good. No one had ever touched him there before, except a couple times at the doctor's office, and the doctor was wearing plastic gloves and was indifferently clinical. Not like this. Not so soft and tender, like he might break. Adam put more lube on his fingers and one of them slipped inside. Chad arched to meet it. The finger penetrated slowly, and Chad flinched at the stretching burn.

Adam whispered to him. "Relax, baby. Push out. Open up for me. Don't clench. It will get better."

He did. As promised, the discomfort eased. Another finger slipped inside, and the pressure of stretching burned more. For a moment Chad thought it might not be worth it, anticipating how much more it would be when it was Adam's cock, not a couple of fingers forcing him open. Then the fingers bent, touched something inside him. His body jerked, legs opened, and his arms flew to grip Adam by the shoulders, and he gasped aloud, his mouth opening wide in shock.

Adam laughed softly. "Feels good, doesn't it?"

Another finger slipped inside. More discomfort, but before Chad could even think to protest, Adam's hand wrapped around his dick and gave a few hard pulls. He ducked his head between Chad's legs. His tongue swirled around the head of his cock and drilled down into his slit.

Chad felt like his eyes crossed. "Holy shit," he gasped and gasped again, his legs dropping open even more to give Adam more room to work his magic.

Adam swallowed his dick whole. The head of his cock hit the back of Adam's throat and slipped down inside. Chad's toes curled. He'd never felt anything like it before. He spread his legs shamelessly and begged for more. Chad had never had head like that before, and he could hear himself practically babbling, making gibberish sounds.

"Nnngghh...g-gonna come," he managed to get out.

Adam pulled off with a wet plop. "Not yet," he said, out of breath. "Hold your legs back, baby," he said.

He pulled his knees back, holding himself open, and lifting his hips to take three fingers.

"T-Too much. Too full."

Adam's mouth licked at him again and shifted, moving up between Chad's welcoming legs. Bracing his weight on one hand, Adam's mesmerizing voice crooned. "Relax, don't fight me. Push out as hard as you can. That's it."

The pressure eased, the fingers withdrew, and Adam guided a new, wet entity to press at his rim. Something big begged for entry, gently, persistently demanding with a rotating stroking. Now or never and Chad tensed again.

"Push out, baby, push out," Adam reminded, his back bowing, to press harder, demanding Chad let him in.

Staring into Adam's eyes, doubt left Chad. He obeyed, relaxing to open himself for what he wanted from the man he wanted. Adam's cock popped past the tight muscles and slipped inside. It hurt. Damn, it hurt and burned, and he grabbed onto Adam's forearms, and his erection sagged. "Oh God, take it out."

"Relax, baby," Adam said, rubbing his free hand seemingly everywhere at once, on Chad's thighs and his chest. "Such a good boy," He punctuated each word with kisses. "You're so good for me. So beautiful. You feel so tight around my cock, baby. Just like velvet. You're my sweet baby."

He pulled hard on Chad's cock while he crooned. The pain eased, and Chad's body stretched, his cock stiffening back up. No one had ever talked to him like that before. The words and tone embarrassed him. At the same time the attention thrilled him. He let go of the clenched muscles protesting the invasion and gradually adjusted to the fullness.

Not moving, Adam waited, letting him relax fully. "Put your legs over my arms," he whispered, waiting again for Chad to comply, lifting Chad's ass a bit higher. Moving slowly, easing in and out, he pulled almost free and slid back in a tender caress. Each time he slid in, he penetrated deeper until his balls brushed softly against Chad's ass cheeks.

With his weight on both his arms, Adam changed his angle of penetration. Each time he moved in or out his cock rubbed directly over the spot his fingers had stroked earlier, the one that made Chad go crazy.

Chad's dick stiffened even more. His breath caught, exhaled in a long "oh" of exquisite pleasure, and he squirmed. He'd never been so excited in his life. He humped up hard against Adam, wanting, needing pressure on his dick. Adam knew what he needed like he always seemed to. He shifted again to free one arm, wrapped his hand around Chad's hard dick, and moved up and down about three times before Chad came with such force he almost bucked Adam off. His eyes shut tight, little stars exploded behind the lids, and he clamped his jaw to keep from screaming out loud.

Adam came right behind him with a loud groan as Chad's body clamped down. When the last groan faded away, he collapsed. He was heavy, pressing down on the back of Chad's thighs, but as long as he could still breathe to catch his breath, Chad didn't mind. He even missed the closeness when Adam pulled free and rolled off to the side. Chad followed him over, not touching, but still wanting to breathe the same air for a moment or two longer.

With a pat on Chad's cheek, Adam sat up on the side of the bed, still catching his breath. Unable to resist, Chad leaned up and put his cheek against Adam's back.

Adam turned around and gave him a shaky smile. "Sweet baby," he murmured softly, pushing himself up. He went into the adjoining bathroom, returning in a few minutes with a warm cloth. "Lie back, baby. I'll clean you up."

He thoroughly wiped down Chad's stomach and thighs, even cleaned his crease, still sticky with lube. The gentle caring gave Chad a warm feeling equal to none he'd ever experienced with a woman. Finished, Adam threw the cloth back on the bathroom floor and flopped down on the bed. Chad wrapped his arms around him, welcoming him back, feeling he couldn't get close enough to him. He nuzzled his face down into Adam's neck and breathed him in.

"I-I never felt like that before," he whispered. "No one ever…"

"I know, baby. Me too," Adam said and held him in his arms until sleep overtook him.

6

Two things were more than apparent to Chad when he woke up, nestled in Adam's arms, both of which caused him to ease away. He liked waking up like this way too much, and he had no business being there. He was a cop on assignment, for God's sake. The last thing on his mind while they fucked was being on the alert for an attack. What the hell was wrong with him?

"Where are you going?"

"We can't do this." He automatically looked for his clothes before he spotted a patch of blue and remembered he hadn't been wearing any.

"I see," Adam said, rolling up to sit on the side of the bed.

"No you don't." Chad stood there, the blue patch of cloth hanging from one finger. "What the hell would have happened last night if we'd been attacked? I was so fucking out of my mind, I wouldn't have known anyone was here until they hit me with a damned stun gun. Or you." He threw his hands in the air. "I've broken one of the cardinal rules. If anyone ever found out, I'd be suspended so fast my head would spin. What the hell was I thinking?"

"About yourself for a change, I should imagine. You've denied your true self—"

"I know, damn it. After last night, I know, but now is not the time or place for it. We can't do that again. That went way the hell beyond practicing to be a sub."

"Okay." Adam walked to the bathroom. "If you'll excuse me, I need to get my shower and dress, or I'm going to be late. As it is, I'll have to forego my workout this morning."

Stung by his coldness, Chad exclaimed, "Okay? What the hell is that? Wham, bam, thank you?"

Adam turned to face him, and the sight of his beautiful body did things

70

to Chad despite the tension. The indifference in his voice ripped into Chad's senses.

"I'm simply agreeing with you."

"You act like you don't even care."

"You've explained the situation. I agree." He shrugged. "I'm just as guilty of forgetting the seriousness of the situation as you are. If you decide to stay, I'll train you, but there won't be any more intimacy between us."

"Fine. I'm glad you understand." Chad said. Hurt even though it didn't make sense to him, he tried damned hard not to show it. "I'm going in to the office. I'll see you this evening."

Chad stormed off to his room, dressed faster than he could ever remember dressing before, and drove off smoking his tires. He was so damned furious, hurt, and confused he could barely think straight and realized it before he reached the office, staying in his car to cool down before he went in. Last night had seemed to answer every question he'd ever had about himself. Everything, absolutely everything, had felt so right. He'd reached heights he never even imagined before and experienced an inner satisfaction that had always been out of reach with a woman. He'd gone to sleep with a different kind of peace and relaxation than he'd ever achieved with anyone else or by giving himself a hand job. Climaxes were just climaxes until it was with someone special, which was what he believed had happened last night. His disappointment in realizing it meant nothing more than a convenient fuck for Adam made him sick to his stomach. How the hell was he supposed to go back there and pretend nothing had happened? Adam had turned his life around and upside down. He'd seduced him into accepting he was gay and then turned his back on him. A little voice in the back of his head said Chad himself was the one who started it, but he pushed the voice aside. He was too hurt to be reasonable.

"Fuck!"

He pounded his fist into the car seat beside him. It wasn't enough. His fist slammed into the dash. Pain shot up his arm, and he fucking deserved it. More than that, he wanted it and punched the dash again.

Chad drove directly home. With skinned knuckles and a swollen hand the best he could do for himself was stay out of sight of everyone. He couldn't believe how fucking stupid he'd been for trusting Adam or messing his hand up in a fit of temper. Sitting with his hand soaking in ice water, he read one of the books from Adam's list. As much as he hated the thought of ever seeing Adam again, he still had a job to do. He'd keep away from Adam the way he planned to start with. He didn't need to practice to know how to act in front of his friends or at the club. Agreeing to it had been no more than a subconscious excuse—it had to be. He had a curiosity. Adam promised to satisfy it. End of story. The man had proven to him he was gay, and even though what he'd thought was happening with Adam wasn't, he still felt relieved. He didn't know what the hell he was going to do about it or where he was going from there, but at least he didn't have to torment himself with wondering anymore.

All his rationalizations didn't lessen the emptiness inside.

Feeling like there was no way in hell he could face Adam again, he picked up his cell to call the chief and admit defeat. He damn near jumped off the couch when it rang in his hand. Looking at the caller ID, he was tempted not to even answer. He'd made up his mind to bail, leaving him no reason to talk to Adam ever again. Maybe once more, to tell him he was through.

"Yeah?"

"Be certain you're there when I return home. I've made arrangements for the meeting this evening."

"Can't wait to get it over with, huh?"

"I believe the sooner this can be brought to an end, the better for all concerned. Don't you agree?"

"Yeah, the sooner the better."

He disconnected without a good-bye. Maybe tonight would garner them results, and he wouldn't have to cry off. God, he hoped so. Adam couldn't be any colder if he were standing in a freezer.

Before he could even work himself into or away from a pity party, his cell rang again.

"Yeah, Johansen , what have you got?"

"A fucking puzzle."

"Excuse me."

"That lead you handed us is going nowhere, thanks to a pile of misinformation. Clarence Rubin did not die a couple of months ago. Try two years, and if he was a closet fag, there's not a sign, not even a hint of it."

Chad flinched at Johansen's insulting use of the word fag, glad again he wasn't in a face to face conversation.

Johansen went on. "I don't know how you expect me to give you any kind of an accurate rundown with inaccurate information."

"So Adam misunderstood. We've got a meeting tonight. I'll get the preacher off to the side and try to get some more details."

"Make sure. I've wasted enough of my time chasing down dead ends."

"That's what you get paid for, asshole. If the father's dead, find out what you can from the mother."

"She's on a fucking vacation and can't be reached, and watch your fucking mouth. I don't have to take any shit off of you."

"I don't have to take any off you, either, just because you keep coming up blank."

For the second time, he disconnected without a good-bye. The case was

72

putting them all on edge. If they didn't get a break soon they might end up beating the shit out of each other.

* * * *

Keeping his distance from Adam, Chad asked, "So how did you arrange it so soon?"

"I traded nights with a colleague, telling him I needed my regular night to prepare for a class."

"He won't think that's suspicious?"

"No, we've traded nights before. Put your jock strap on under your jeans, the red one, I think. That will prevent the need for you to do more than strip when we return for drinks."

"I'm not comfortable with the idea of prancing around in front of your friends with only my cock and balls covered."

"I told you what to expect."

"You also told me I set limits. I'm not going down to only a scrap of cloth covering my balls in front of strangers."

"Oh, for God's sake, leave your shirt on then, unbuttoned."

Chad walked off without agreeing. He paused for a split second when he could have sworn he heard the word, "Big baby…" trailing after him. With the bad memories that word brought up, he ignored it, but he could feel his face burning as he put the red jock on, pulling a pair of the new jeans Adam bought over it. He looked for the longest shirt among the new ones Adam bought. He might or might not strip, depending on how totally pissed off he got before they got back here. Really not caring anymore, he suspected he might be defiant or at least behaving spitefully.

The drive to the church was silent. Neither man spoke. Once they reached the large room with chairs arranged in a circle, Chad sat down beside Adam. He listened with sympathy to the miserable comments of the young men, some no more than teenagers, kicked out of their homes for their sexual preferences. Hearing their stories, he was almost glad he'd never been brave enough to admit to his early fascination, though he hoped his parents wouldn't have been that cold-hearted and cruel. He'd find out soon enough when he broke the news to them.

After an hour and a half the group broke up. Adam moved off to speak to his friend, Benjamin. Chad took advantage of the break by joining the pastor at the refreshment table.

"Nice group," he commented.

"Some very fine young men," Jason agreed.

"Do you know them personally or have you just met them here?"

"Met them here. Word has gone out on the street that they're welcome, though the basement is running out of room for cots. I'm working on building a group home where they will have a safe place to live until they can find jobs and support themselves. We're raising money for it now, actually. Any donation for the cause would be greatly appreciated."

"Sorry, I don't have my checkbook with me." That guy at the club had been right. The preacher didn't miss a chance to put the squeeze on somebody. "Have you lived here all your life?"

"No, only the last few years steadily. My father moved us around a lot as children. I guess that made me a nomad. I had some difficulty deciding where I wanted settle. I finished my theology courses here and made enough friends and contacts that I've stayed."

"From what I hear you were lucky to find affordable living."

"Not at all. My mother has property here. I've taken advantage of that."

"Oh, that's right. Adam mentioned you lived with your brother."

"Yes."

A pained expression said more than words on that subject, but Chad didn't let up. "I think he said you'd lost your father a couple of months ago. My condolences."

"Thank you. His loss was extremely difficult for me. We had been estranged since I was a child. I had never given up on reconciliation."

Adam hadn't made a mistake on the time. Since it was pretty unlikely the preacher did, Chad suspected the man might be lying. Why he would puzzled him.

Jason sighed dramatically. "My brother never wished to reconnect. I must say as disappointing as my failure to reach him each time he's here, it's always a relief when he leaves."

Chad only nodded at that statement, still determined to dig. "If I remember right, Adam said the problem—"

Adam gripped Chad by the elbow. "It's time to leave."

"I was just—"

"Now," he ordered, his fingers pressing against his arm. "My friends are waiting."

Torn between obeying the way he should to keep in character and wanting more information, Chad dropped his eyes. The objective for the evening was to convince any watchers they were a happy couple. "Yes, Sir. I'm coming."

Adam turned on his heel. Chad followed, hating every fucking minute of it. He didn't speak until they were in the privacy of the car and driving down the road. Adam's continuing coolness toward him had Chad frustrated and jittery, not to mention totally pissed off, shoving the job to the back of his mind. He wasn't given the opportunity to find out anything new anyway, not with Adam playing big, bad Dom without listening to what he'd tried to tell him.

After the huge thing that had happened between them last night, how could Adam not talk to him about it? Didn't he realize how freaked out he was? How badly he wanted reassurances from him, wanted to talk about it? It was like a big pink elephant between them, and the thing was about to crowd him right out of the car. Had the son of a bitch just used him as a booty call? His face burned at the idea, and he gripped his knees until his knuckles were white.

"What the hell is the hurry?" Chad asked.

"We were ready to leave."

"Yeah, you may have been, but I needed to talk to that preacher and get some details straight. This is an investigation, you know. If you weren't so worried about your precious image, I might have found out something that would help us pin these murders on that brother of his."

"It's my precious image you're banking on to pull him out in the open. Don't forget that."

"I doubt any one even noticed me moving over to talk to the preacher until you made an issue of it."

"They noticed, Chad. We always leave immediately to avoid Rubin." He barely paused to add, "Just because you re-thought what happened last night is no reason—"

Chad twisted in the seat to face him and cut him off, by exploding. "I re-thought it?" he shouted. "You're the one who turned into a fucking ice machine!"

"You made the excuse to pull away, and I only—"

"It wasn't a fucking excuse! I jeopardized the entire operation because of my attraction to you!"

"Stop shouting at me. I won't tolerate that."

"Fuck what you won't tolerate! I'll be your damned puppet in public, but you don't tell me how to act in private!"

"Are you asking for punishment, Chad? Is that what this is?"

"Yeah, like what? Another spanking like when I was too out of my head to even know what was going on?"

"So you claim. Maybe the drug simply took away your crippling inhibitions, and you were able to experience an honest reaction for the first time in your life."

Chad twisted around and flopped back in the seat. "I wasn't inhibited last night. That was as honest as I could make it."

Adam glanced at him and then quickly away. Chad clamped his jaw shut. They drove for another block with neither of them speaking until Adam finally broke the silence. "I had no intentions of becoming involved with you. You're too inexperienced, volatile, obstinate…"

"Yeah, yeah, everything you hate."

Adam continued as if not interrupted. "…unwilling to even admit to who you really are."

"I admitted to being gay!"

"Afraid to completely submit yourself…"

"I get it. You hate everything about me."

"Shut up, Chad, and allow me to finish." He waited half a beat and when Chad didn't respond, continued. "When you said what you did this morning, I thought it was for the best."

By then Chad's stomach was in a knot. His breathing rate had kicked up to equal someone running a mile, and he felt like a hand gripped him by the throat.

"I am, however, committed to this situation. I'll do my best and expect you to do the same."

"Fine. Like I said, I'll be your puppet in public, but not in private."

"Fine."

"I fucking hate you," he retorted, sounding like a child and knowing it.

A long silence developed between them, and it was becoming more and more awkward.

"I'm sorry you feel that way," Adam said quietly.

They rode silently for another block or two, the air thick between them. Finally, in self-defense, Chad changed the subject. "Rubin said again that his father died two months ago, but records show it was two years ago. Why would he lie about it?"

"For attention."

"That was a pretty fast answer."

"I've suspected for some time that Rubin is one of those people who like to be the center of attention. He uses sympathy to get it."

Chad grunted. "The poor me ploy?"

"The woman you saw giving him attention after the funeral wasn't the only one who does, and you've seen how the men at the meeting treat him, like a martyred saint."

"What happened two months ago then?"

Adam shrugged. "Attention was waning possibly, that and his brother showed up."

"It keeps coming back to his brother." He lapsed into silence, mulling the possibilities over. "Has anyone else in your lifestyle met the brother?"

"Not that I know of. I can ask this evening if I can work it into the conversation, without arousing suspicion."

"So everyone is still coming to your house?"

"Yes, they are. I have a couple of nice bottles of Bordeaux…"

"Wine? Seriously?"

Adam gave him another irritated glance. "For God's sake, Chad, we all have to get to work in the morning. Yes, wine." Adam glanced over at him. "We'll have couple of glasses and some of the cheese I left out on the counter."

"Oh, how sophisticated of us," he retorted, remembering his anger. "I guess I'm the waitress."

Appearing to not hear his sarcastic tone, Adam nodded. "While everyone is settling in, and I'm opening the wine, go to the kitchen and get the crystal cheese tray from the cabinet by the sink. Arrange the cheese on the plate and add some of the small crackers I left out too. Then bring out the tray and offer it around. When you finish, leave it on the coffee table and sit by me."

"When you say, 'offer it around,' I assume you mean offer it to the Doms, right?"

Adam blew out a breath. "You don't have to be so sarcastic, damn it. No, Chad. This is a casual get together, not a scene at the club. Their partners will be sitting next to them. Simply hold the tray out in front of both of them, but remember not to make unnecessary eye contact with the Doms. I've always been pretty strict in the past with my subs, and they'll notice if things are too different with you. Really, this is not that difficult, Chad. A trained monkey could do it."

Stung by his words, Chad bristled and knew Adam meant it to chaff at him. Neither said anything further for several miles before Chad asked another question, his mood still belligerent. "What about what I'm wearing? This strap? You said to wear this damn thing in front of your friends. Should I do a striptease right there in the living room while you hum a little music, or should I wait until I go back to my cage like a good monkey?"

Adam shot him an angry look and pressed his lips tightly together. "Must you be so impertinent, Chad? We're the ones being threatened, you know, and we've already lost several of our good friends. I'm sorry if I hurt your feelings."

The words would have probably gone a long way to cool Chad's temper if Adam hadn't tacked on that last little bit.

"You still haven't answered my impertinent question. What do I do about my clothes?"

"Oh for God's sake..." Adam seemed to deliberately calm himself before he continued. "When you go inside, go to your room, and take off your pants, shoes, and socks, and unbutton your shirt. The back of your shirt should come down long enough to preserve your damn modesty. Does that suit you?"

"Suits me just fine. Sir."

"You need to lose the attitude, Chad, if we're to pull this off. It'll be the first time my friends are around you for any length of time. Personally, I don't suspect any of them, but word does get around. The idea, according to your chief, is to make this look real, and to be as visible as possible. We're supposed to be attracting attention."

"Don't worry about me, Professor. I know how to do my job. I know this is all just a sham, but we have to make it look good." He stared straight ahead, ignoring the sharp look Adam gave him and refusing to make eye contact.

They reached Adam's house and pulled the car into the garage. Adam got out and went to the front door to greet his friends as they arrived, while Chad went in through the kitchen door in the garage. He went to the guest room and took off his shoes and socks, then slid off the new jeans, folded them carefully, and left them on the bed. Taking his time, he went into the bathroom, relieved himself and washed his hands, then stood looking in the mirror while he slowly unbuttoned the shirt. He hardly recognized himself.

The red jock strap was shockingly bright against his pale skin. Adam had been right. The woven pouch in front lifted his cock and balls, making him look huge. They were so brief if he got a hard-on, his cock would be peeking over the band. Not much chance of that, the way he currently felt about Adam. The shirt would help some. Made of silky material, long-sleeved, with a tail long enough to reach the top of his thighs, it covered his bare ass completely. Of course, with it unbuttoned, it had a tendency to drift away from his body in the breeze as he walked, but he made a mental note to hold onto it whenever he could.

Deciding he was as ready as he'd ever be, and he'd dawdled as long as he could, he left his room and went directly to the kitchen, looking into the living room as he passed through. Four of the same men who had been at the club that horrible night were the guests. Knowing their names did not make Chad feel any more comfortable around them. Adam sat alone on the love seat, pouring glasses of wine, while Cole was on the sofa, his partner Sam lounging against him. Benjamin, the Dom of the other couple, sat in the big armchair, with Paul, his sub, sitting between his feet, his back against his partner's legs. Benjamin was leaning forward, drinking a glass of wine and telling some story that had them all smiling, with an arm draped casually over Paul's bare chest. Benjamin was the one planning on doing a scene the night Chad ended up in a private room minutes away from being raped. Cole was the one who warned Adam. He could like Cole. Benjamin on the other hand grated on his nerves.

Chad wasn't the only one who had undressed, to a degree at least, for the occasion. Both of the other subs had their shirts unbuttoned. Sam had slipped off his shoes and unzipped his pants. It was hard to miss Cole's hand disappearing under the waistband of his underwear.

Not exactly like any get together he'd ever been to. Dorothy, you really aren't in Kansas anymore. He went quickly into the kitchen but felt someone's gaze on him and glanced back over his shoulder to see all the men in the room staring at him. Self-consciously, he opened up the cabinet and got down the heavy crystal cheese tray and put out the block of cheese and the funny little knife beside it. Chad held the knife up, studying it. It might have been a commonly used utensil in Adam's world, but not in his home growing up in rural Georgia. In a crazy way, the little knife seemed to underscore the disparity between them. Though not so terribly obvious on the surface, it was in the details where the difference lay.

Chad cut off quite a few slices and arranged them nicely on the outside edge of the tray, stalling for time. Finally, he added the crackers in the middle, and there were no more excuses for him to stay in the kitchen.

Holding the tray out in front of him with both hands, he walked slowly back into the living room, feeling the breeze taking the flimsy shirt and drift it out behind him, exposing his ass. With his face blazing, for the first time he thought of one real advantage for a sub in lowering his gaze. He walked first to Cole and Sam, holding the tray out to them and waiting for Cole to select what he wanted. Shit, he'd forgotten the napkins, but then he saw that a stack was on the coffee table. Adam must have figured he'd forget them.

He glanced up at Adam and saw him watching his every move. It made him so nervous he stumbled over Paul's foot, but righted himself and held the tray down for Benjamin and Paul, reminding himself at the last minute to not look directly at the Dom, but not before he's seen the small smirk on Benjamin's face. What the hell was that about? He thought he'd done pretty well except for the one little blunder.

Making his way over to Adam, he held the tray out. Adam took some slices and put them on a napkin. "Put the tray on the coffee table, Pet, and have a seat."

He did and sank gratefully down beside Adam, furious at himself for the little thrill that went through him when Adam immediately put an arm around him, and drew him back against his chest. He held his wine glass to Chad's lips, and Chad took a small sip, trying not to make a face when the dry, red wine hit his tongue. He hated wine and always had.

He jumped though, when Adam's other hand snaked around to the front of his jock strap and dipped inside. Adam's warm hand closed around his shaft, and Chad sucked in a breath, glancing around to see if anyone noticed. Only Paul stared back at him with a knowing little smile.

The Doms talked, mostly having to do with their classes, giving Chad the idea they were deliberately avoiding the murders. After a few minutes of Adam's treatment, Chad zoned out, trying like hell not to respond to the blood rushing to his cock as Adam continued to caress him. He only held him gently, his thumb moving in little circles over the head of his prick, but occasionally, he dipped that thumb into Chad's slit, making Chad's stomach muscles contract. During the massage, Adam continued to press the glass to his lips, forcing him to take more, and even the sips, on his empty stomach, soon made him feel warm and loose-limbed. The thumb slipped into his slit again and Chad's head felt too heavy to hold up. He let it drop back on

Adam's shoulder.

His soft sounds as Adam played with him must have become too loud, because Adam whispered "Shh…" to him in his ear. He pulled the wicked hand away, making Adam sigh quietly in relief, but then his hand reappeared on Chad's thigh. He nudged his thighs apart and slipped his hand down to the juncture of his thighs and his pelvic bone, rubbing hard in a little circle under his balls. Chad let out a breathy grunt and looked up to see several pairs of eyes watching him.

Before he had a chance to become self-conscious, Adam whispered, "Kiss me," in his ear. Unable to resist him, he angled his head farther back, and Adam caught his mouth in a hungry kiss.

Across from them, Benjamin laughed softly. "You're right about him, Adam. Once you have him completely trained, he'll be something quite special. He has such a straight boy look that watching him submit to you will be sweet. Why don't you let him and Paul do a scene at the club this weekend? Once they get each other worked up, we could step in for the finale." He pronounced the word like in French, fee-nahl-uh, with the emphasis on the middle syllable.

Pretentious ass.

Adam slipped his hand inside Chad's waistband again, going to his balls and giving them a nice massage. In another minute, Chad was going to spurt cum all over the front of his jock strap if Adam kept it up. Damn him.

"No, he's not ready yet. I don't know if I'll ever want to share him actually."

Thank God for that.

"Really?" Benjamin said. "Don't tell me you're going to become possessive and selfish, like Cole here."

Apparently this was an old argument, because Cole simply smiled and kept right on fingering Sam, or doing whatever it was his hand was doing in his jeans. Sam was lying in his lap by then, his jeans pushed down low on his hips, and his eyes practically rolled back in his head.

"Not all of us are quite as exhibitionist as you, Benjamin. Sam and I don't like performing scenes at the club. We do perfectly fine without it." Cole's voice was languid and soft.

Chad wondered what the hell Cole thought he was doing now. Not an exhibitionist? He was practically giving his boyfriend a hand job right there on the sofa in front of all of them. As was Adam with him, come to think of it.

"Leave him alone, Benjamin," Adam said, smiling. "Take care of your own boy."

Benjamin glanced down at him and leaned over to give Paul an openmouthed, wet kiss. Embarrassed, Chad turned his face toward Adam's chest, his unease at the openness of the people in the room growing. If some kind of orgy was about to start up, Adam could count him out. He could hear the soft, wet sucking sounds of the kiss across from him and Paul making low moans. Adam kissed the top of Chad's head and snuggled him in closer, apparently realizing how uncomfortable he was getting.

Benjamin came up for air. "Maybe I'll just take him home and take care of him since you both have early classes tomorrow."

"Speaking of which, I hate to be a bad host, but I really do have an early morning," Adam said. Chad sagged in relief.

Both couples prepared to leave, slipping on shoes, rearranging their clothing and draining their wine glasses. Adam pushed Chad gently away and rose to his feet. While he was still bantering with Benjamin and walking his guests to the door, Chad gathered up the wine glasses and soiled napkins, taking them into the kitchen. It was hard to walk with the massive erection he had, but he gritted his teeth, determined Adam shouldn't know. Like he could miss the huge bulge in the jock strap. Chad made another trip for the cheese tray, curious as to the low voices he heard in the foyer as he returned to the kitchen. He was rinsing glasses to put in the dishwasher, keeping his groin turned toward the sink, when Adam came back in the kitchen. Before either could say a word, a loud pounding took them both at a run to the door.

Adam barely turned the knob before Cole shoved the door open. "This was on my windshield." He waved a sheet of paper in Adam's face. "There's one on Benjamin's too."

* * * *

Adam seemed to be lost in his thoughts, drumming his fingers nervously against the arm of his chair. All Chad could think of was those chilling words on the notes tucked under the windshield wipers. I gave you fair warning. Retribution is near.

Bring it, you sick son of a bitch. He clenched and unclenched his fists. He'd like to get his hands on the asshole for about five minutes. It would be all he'd need. They found the same note to Adam stuck in his mailbox.

They'd called the police, dialing nine-one-one, and keeping to their cover. Chad barely had time to slip back into jeans before a patrol car hit the curb. Phillips and Johansen arrived after the patrol officers contacted them and wanted names of everyone who had been at the group session to hunt down and interview, theorizing that someone had followed them from the church. They'd interview Preacher Rubin, too. With the new notes, the killer had given them a connection to the church to justify it and wouldn't serve as a warning to Jeremy.

Chad kept his mouth shut until the frightened guest went home. Once they were gone, he turned on Philips and Johansen. "How the hell did he get by the surveillance team?"

Philips answered. "They were following you in case this guy changes his MO. They had to stay behind the other two cars and hold back until they were sure you were all inside. They didn't get back into position soon enough is all we can figure. It was just dumb ass luck he wasn't spotted."

"What about the cameras?"

"Some guy all dressed in black, baseball cap pulled down over his face and collar turned up. We know he was here, but it's too vague to get an ID from."

"Double the team. I want someone on Adam at all times and someone watching this house when he's gone. That bastard could have come in and been waiting for us."

"I'll talk to the chief about it."

"It's not negotiable."

"Calm down, Williams, I'll pass that on. It'll be up to the chief. You know that. Did you pick up anything new tonight?"

"Only that the family moved around a lot, and he repeated that his father died a couple of months ago. I didn't have time to dig any deeper." He shot a look at Adam to remind him why and tipped his head in his direction. "Adam thinks he's one of those sympathy addicts and lies for attention."

"Why?" Philips asked.

"Just a feeling he gives me," Adam answered. "Hearing he's lied about his past doesn't surprise me. He glories in the attention he gets when he's telling people how he's suffered and how righteous he is. Why are you interested in his father if the man's already dead, regardless of when?"

"Motive," Chad explained. "The profiler thinks the killer could be taking his rage against his father out on similar men."

"Was his father a college professor?"

"Insurance salesman," Philips answered.

"Was he gay?"

"Not that we could find."

"Then why is he killing gay college professors?"

All three men stared at him for a moment. "Fuck if I know," Philips retorted.

"Maybe one sexually abused him," Johansen suggested.

Adam gave him an incredulous look, rolled his eyes and stood up. "I hate to be rude, gentlemen, but it's late. I have an early class in the morning. Stay if you like, but I'm going to bed."

The detectives cleared out quickly after that, leaving them alone. Adam disappeared into his bedroom. The whole ordeal with the police had taken over two hours, and Chad was tired both physically and emotionally. He finished what he'd been doing when it all started and put the last glass into the dishwasher before turning back around to see Adam standing with his hands shoved in his pockets, just watching him. It startled him, since he thought Adam was already in bed.

"You did well tonight, Chad. Very convincing."

"Thanks." Chad stared steadily back at him, determined to not be the one to drop his gaze first, but finally unable to hold it in the face of Adam's steady regard. He sighed and dropped his gaze to the floor. "I'm going to call the station. See if they got any prints or anything on those notes."

Adam nodded. "I'm going on to bed then. I…uh…I'll see you in the morning or after I get home, whatever."

"Sure." Don't worry, asshole, I get it. You don't want me in your bed tonight. No problem. Well, shit, I shouldn't be there anyway.

Adam started to leave but then turned back to him. "Look, I don't want this to be awkward between us. Last night was…"

"A mistake," Chad said in a cool tone. "I get it. Don't worry about it."

Adam's eyes darkened, but he turned on his heel and took a couple of steps down the hallway, before pausing and looking over his shoulder. Not making eye contact, he said, "You know every man in the room wanted you tonight. I could see it in their eyes."

He turned and left. Chad listened for the bedroom door to close before he turned off the lights and went to the guest room. If Adam wanted this to be over between them, then why the hell did he say things like that to him? Every man in the room wanted him? He could truthfully say no one had ever said those words to him before tonight.

Feeling hurt and angry he fell down on top of the covers on the bed and stared up at the ceiling for a long time, trying to make his mind a blank, but it wasn't working. After what was probably the most intense sexual experience of his life the night before, he didn't know how he was supposed to be feeling. Once he'd convinced himself he was gay and definitely attracted to Adam, suddenly Adam wanted to distance himself from him in every way that had nothing to do with the case—except he kept giving out mixed signals. That annoying part of his mind that kept intruding on his thoughts reminded him he was the one who started the whole distance thing, but he firmly told it to shut the hell up.

He didn't want to think about how Adam's hands had felt on him earlier or how much he wanted to be in the bedroom lying beside him. The sex between them must have meant nothing more or less than Adam playing around with a new toy the night before—which happened to be him.

As late as it was, he decided to wait until morning to call the station and just go to bed. There was little chance they'd get the notes processed before then. He undressed and put on a pair of his old underwear and fell back on the bed. Two hours later he awoke to his cell phone ringing insistently in the dark.

He struggled to come awake and find it, trying hard to get his eyes open enough to see. What had ended up being at least a full glass of wine had relaxed him enough that he'd fallen into a deep sleep, so that he mumbled "Williams," into the phone and then had to repeat it when the voice on the other end, said, "Hello? Hello?"

"This is Williams," he growled. "Who is this?"

"This is Sgt. Bailey from nine-one-one." Waking up a little more, he recognized her voice. She was graveyard shift supervisor, a nice lady in her forties who was attractive in a comfortable, motherly way. She was also really sharp and competent. "Sorry to wake you Corporal Williams, but Sgt. Johansen wanted us to call you. There's been a murder, sir, and I'm sorry to have to be the one to tell you, but it's Sgt. Phillips."

"What?" he shouted into the phone, wide awake in an instant. "What are you talking about?"

"The officers on the scene say he must have walked in on the killer. He was at the home of some people from the University. Some of the ones he'd taken a report from earlier. From what the officers have been able to piece together, he had some further questions for his report. He said he wanted to double check something and doubted they'd be asleep yet. He sent Sgt. Johansen home and never called for backup. We started getting calls about shots fired from the neighbors. We couldn't raise him on the radio, and officers were dispatched to the scene. They found him inside the residence, fatally wounded. He died on the scene before they could take him to the hospital."

A sick, sour feeling rose from the pit of Chad's stomach. Almost afraid to ask, he said, "Whose home was it, Sgt. Bailey?"

"Benjamin LeCroy and Samuel Rosser."

"Oh God," he said softly, feeling the bile at the back of his throat. "Tell Johansen I'm on my way."

"No, sir, he said to tell you to stay put. He'll talk to you first thing in the morning, as soon as he gets more information."

Chad took a deep breath, trying to calm down. "LeCroy and Rosser, were they...?

"They weren't hurt at all. They didn't arrive home until it was all over. They stopped for something to eat after leaving your location. Most of it's guess work so far, but they think Sgt. Phillips saw something suspicious and went to check or was ambushed when he approached the property. It appears he was shot outside the residence, though his body was found inside, and his service weapon is missing. That's about all the information I have now."

"Thanks, Bailey. Thanks for calling." He hung up and got dressed quickly. Johansen wanted him to stay put, so security measures both here and at the other houses must be thin after what happened. Probably most of the patrol officers were at the crime scene. Shit, how did this keep happening? He felt like he was about to shatter into pieces. He wanted to put his fist through a wall or kick something. He debated over telling Adam and decided he should. He'd be angry if Chad didn't wake him.

He went down the hall and knocked on Adam's door. He expected Adam to call out to come in, and startled when the door quickly opened up. "Chad? What is it? What's happened?"

"I-uh-I came to tell you about your friends, Benjamin and Sam…"

Adam's face blanched of color, and he took a step back. "Oh my God, are they…?"

"No, no, they're okay. The killer was at their house though, apparently waiting for them to come home. Sgt. Phillips—you remember him, right? Older guy, about sixty, with gray hair?"

"Yes, of course."

"He was outside waiting for them to come home so he could ask a few more questions for his report. They're not sure of details as yet, he must have noticed something suspicious, went to investigate. Someone shot him. He never called for backup." Feeling like he was about to explode, Chad slammed his fist into the door beside him. "Shit! Why didn't he call for backup?"

Adam grabbed his arm and held on, not trying to stop him, but perhaps trying to soothe him or calm him down. Chad looked at Adam, feeling tears prickling the back of his eyes. "He was shot, Adam. Shot and left for dead inside the residence. He died at the scene a few minutes later. The killer suckered us. He fucking suckered us, calling all the attention to here and leaving them exposed."

Adam pulled him into his arms and helped him over to the bed to sit down. Chad resisted at first, but Adam was insistent, making soothing noises to him as he led him to the bed.

"He was going to retire in six months. Already had a camper bought for him and his wife. He was going to go fishing every day, he said. Maybe take along the grandkids. Did I tell you he had three grandkids?"

"Shh…don't think about it anymore now, baby. Just try to relax a minute."

"He was doing his job, though. Can't say he wasn't doing his job. He probably fucking saved Benjamin and Paul, you know? If he hadn't been there, they would've walked right in on the killer."

"I know, baby. He was a brave officer."

"Damn straight he was. But why in the hell didn't he call for backup?" He slammed his fist down onto the mattress beside him again and jumped back up to his feet. "Goddamn it, he knew better than that."

"Chad, you need to calm down."

"It was Jeremy. I fucking know it. Damn it, why did that sick fuck have to kill him? He was going to kill both of them, you know, both Benjamin and Paul, and they were sitting in the living room tonight, right across from us."

"I know, baby."

"Is it because they're gay? Is that it? So their lives—the lives of all those men who were killed held less value somehow? Someone thought they didn't have the right to love who and how they wanted to, enough to kill them for it. Are you kidding me?"

Adam caught hold of his arm. "Chad, listen to me. I want to help you, but you have to let this go."

"How can I let it go? How can I? I'm a police officer, Adam. Sworn to protect and serve. Well, how the hell did I do that tonight, huh? You tell me."

"Chad. Be quiet."

He turned his head toward Adam wonderingly. "What?"

"Be quiet and listen to me. Do you trust me?"

"What? What are you talking about?"

"You're falling apart, Chad. Let me help you."

Chad shook his head and wrapped his arms around himself, shivering. "You know what one of the last things Phillips said to me when they gave me this assignment? He said this case was giving him an education. He made a little joke about cock cages." He laughed and even he could hear the hysteria in it. "Pretty good, huh?"

"Listen to me and shut up," Adam said sternly, pulling Chad around to face him. "Stand up and take off your clothes."

"I…why do you want me to…"

"Just do it. Now, with no more questions."

Chad got to his feet almost in a daze, but slowly unbuttoned his shirt. Adam watched him steadily, as he took off his shirt and then his pants, urging him on firmly when he hesitated. When he'd stripped completely down, Adam directed him to the long, leather upholstered bench at the foot of the bed. Chad had never really noticed before how tall the bench was, almost even with the top of the raised footboard. He would actually have to hoist up his hips a bit to sit on it.

"Sit down here on this, and I'll be right back."

Chad eased up onto the bench, and found that only the tips of his toes were still in contact with the floor. He sat quietly until Adam returned, holding a length of rope in his hands and a bottle of water. He nodded at Chad as he came up to him. "Lay down on your back, Chad. I'm taking control."

* * * *

86

Those weren't the only things he brought over to the bench. On his way back into the bedroom, Adam stopped by the chest of sex toys by the door in his bedroom.

As he straightened up from digging in the chest, Chad looked up at him with a puzzled frown. "What are you doing, Adam?"

"From this point on, you call me Sir. Understood?"

"Uh…"

"Is that understood?"

Chad shook his head. "C'mon, Adam. I'm not in the mood for this."

Adam stepped beside him and took his hair in his hands, jerking his head back to look up into Adam's eyes.

"I told you to call me Sir. Did I stutter?"

"No. Okay. Sir. Is that better?"

"Lie down on your back, boy, feet on the floor. Do it."

Chad lay down with only one more sullen look at him. Chad had never been easy, never been compliant. Adam was taking a chance with him, but he thought he knew what Chad needed, and he had to be the one to give it to him.

He positioned Chad so that he was on his back, his ass right at the end of the bench, his legs hanging awkwardly. "Chad," he said softly as he folded his arms over his chest. "I'm going to tie you down, but I won't leave you for a second, okay? I'm right here with you, and I'll take care of you. You trust me?" He wound the rope over his chest and arms and then back under the bench. He brought it back over his waist and then his thighs.

"Y-Yeah, but I don't understand. What if Johansen comes over?"

"It's three o'clock in the morning, Chad. No one is coming over. We're alone, and I'm in charge. Understand?"

"I understand, I guess, but what are you doing, Sir?" Chad's voice sounded so young and confused Adam stopped to drop a kiss on his forehead and smooth his hair back from it.

"I'm taking care of you, baby. I'm going to help you. You need to realize you're not at fault because you're not in charge of the whole fucking world. You're not even in control here, are you?"

Adam finished tying Chad down by wrapping the ropes around his calves and pulling his ankles back tightly against the legs of the bench, spreading and securing them, leaving his crotch open. He stood up to survey his handiwork. "Very nice. Very sweet." He noticed approvingly. Chad's cock was stiff and hard. On some level, his body was approving of what was happening.

He stripped off his pajama pants and stood naked by the bench. Chad watched him every second. He gripped Chad's shaft and pumped it slowly up and down. A sharp intake of breath came from Chad's lips as he finally seemed to realize just what his situation was.

"Chad," Adam said softly. "You have to let go of all of this. All of the guilt and the terror and the anxiety you're feeling. I'm going to take it from you, all of it. In return, you're going to give me your control. Understand?"

"I-uh…"

"You no longer are in control. Try to get up, Chad." He watched as Chad wiggled a little in the ropes. "You can't do anything I don't let you do from this point on. Your power is gone, baby. It's history, and I'm taking over."

"No," Chad shook his head. "No, this is crazy. Let me go."

"Submit to me, boy. You need to learn a few lessons, and I'm going to be the one to teach you. Not every decision depends on you, baby. As a matter of fact, nothing depends on you here. Not when you're submitting to me, because now it's all about me and what I want, and you're going to give it to me."

Chad's eyes grew wider as if he suddenly realized how helpless he really was. He struggled in his bonds, first just a little and then violently, but he was too securely tied to hurt himself or do much more than exhaust himself. Finally, panting for breath, he looked up at Adam, his pupils blown and his face red. "Please."

"Please what, baby? What is it you want? You can't get out of this with your strength and you can't talk your way out of it, but you don't have to worry. You trust me. You know I'd never harm you. Isn't that right?"

Chad nodded, raising his head and trying to look down his body toward his dick, which was still being firmly jacked by Adam's hand. Drops of pearly pre cum glistened on the head, and he groaned.

"Words, baby. Tell me you trust me."

"I-I trust you, Sir. I do, but I need to get up. Please let me up."

"No. I like you right where you are. Right here where I can take whatever I want."

Chad's head fell back with a groan, but his cock was even harder, if possible. "Tell me your safe words, Chad."

"Uh, my safe words? You mean the red and yellow thing?"

"Yes, baby. Very good. Are those your words?"

Adam fondled his balls, and Chad dropped his head back on the bench, breathing hard. "Yes, Sir. I guess so. Can I say red now? Please?"

"You can if you really want to. We haven't even really started yet, though. Are you sure you want to?"

"Yes…no…no, I don't want to."

Adam could see that Chad still considered this as a contest of wills. He had to realize what it really was and submit to him. He had to break him down first. It was the only way to then put his boy back together again.

"There's no need to be embarrassed, baby. There's only you and me here. Put this in my hands and let me take care of you. Realize that you belong to me now. All you can do is to submit to me. Do you submit, baby boy? Do you give me all the control?"

Chad looked up at him and sighed. "I can put it all in your hands? I don't have to do anything?" Adam heard the longing in his voice, and it made a strange butterfly feeling start up in his chest. The short talk he'd had with Cole before they left the first time had helped put some things in perspective for Adam.

"Yes, baby. Nothing you can do anyway. So of course, you can put it in my hands. I'm taking it all from you. I'll take care of you, just like I did the other night. You're mine, aren't you?"

"Y-Yes, Sir."

Adam smiled, pleased that Chad was finally submitting properly, finally beginning to let go. If he didn't lose some of this rigid control and anxiety, it was going to consume him and tear him apart.

He bent down to lick the pre-cum from the head of Chad's shaft, and Chad stiffened into a human rod. "Oh God, I'm going to come."

"No, you won't, because I haven't given you permission. You belong to me, and you can't do anything I don't allow you to do." He pulled out a cock ring from the supplies he'd gathered earlier and slipped it over Chad's balls and onto his shaft.

Chad raised his head again to look and then fell back, panting. Adam leaned over his face to make eye contact with him, and he looked back up with a different expression on his face. "Thank you, Sir," he said, and Adam hummed approvingly.

"That's right, baby. I'm taking care of you. Now where was I?" He bent back down and licked up the length of Chad's shaft to the tip and with a sudden motion, swallowed him down, deep throating him. Holding Chad's cock at the base, he bobbed his head up and down, enjoying the interesting noises Chad was making.

He moved around to where Chad's ass hung almost off the bench, his legs spread apart and open for him. He spread Chad's cheeks apart, circled his rim with his tongue, and stuck it in and out of his little pink hole over and over until Chad was babbling and incoherent. It sounded a little like he was begging to come, and Adam pulled away for a moment to allow him to recover a little. When his cries changed to little mewling sounds, Adam returned to eating him out, and listened as he fell apart all over again.

When his cries had grown truly frantic, Adam stopped and came around to his head. He leaned over and kissed him. "Did you want to ask me something, sweet boy?"

"Oh, God, please. Please fuck me, Sir. Please, please let me come."

"Mm, you beg so pretty. Tell me first, baby. Who's in charge here?"

"Y-You are. You are, Sir."

"And whose baby are you?"

"You're-you're in charge, Sir."

"Whose baby are you? Say it, Chad. Who do you belong to?"

Chad's eyes grew even wider, and he shook his head, "No," he groaned. "Please don't make me say that."

"No? Then I'm afraid you haven't earned it yet, boy." He looked down at Chad's cock, rigid and a dark, angry red in his cock ring, leaking copious amounts of pre-cum. He slapped his cock hard with an open hand. Chad's head shot up, and he yelled something Adam couldn't understand.

Adam went back around to his perfect little ass, and drawing back his hand, he slapped Chad's balls, right to left, again and again, while Chad bucked his hips and yelled curses at him.

"No, stop! You bastard, stop it! Let me out of this shit, now!"

"Be quiet, boy. You know your safe word. If you really want me to stop, use it. Go on, say it." He paused and waited while Chad whimpered and looked away. "That's what I thought. Now be quiet like a good boy."

He struck at his balls again with an open hand, and finally, as he continued to strike them, with an occasional slap at his dick, only deep grunts came from Chad's throat.

Adam stopped and gently petted and massaged them. Chad shuddered and sobbed softly. "All your pleasure and your pain come from me, baby. I can give you whatever I want, because you belong to me. Understand?"

"Y-Yes, Sir," Chad sobbed.

His erection had flagged, so Adam took his cock again, holding the shaft in his hand and moving it slowly up and down until it started to thicken back up. Chad tried to arch into his touch, wanting more, harder.

Adam picked up an anal plug and lubed it well, then eased it into Chad's hole, wiggling it gently and pushing it past the first tight ring of muscle. It wasn't a large plug, but he wanted Chad to be ready for him when the time came, and he wanted him nice and stretched out. Chad never complained, never even groaned all through the insertion, and Adam spoke softly to him. "Such a good boy for me."

Chad sighed.

Adam came back around to his head and kissed him for a long time, open mouthed, sloppy kisses that left Chad breathing hard. He played with his nipples as he was kissing him and then moved to take each one of them in his mouth, kissing and biting them until Chad arched up again against the ropes.

"Ready to admit you're my baby, Chad? Ready to admit you belong to me?"

Chad bit his lip and stubbornly turned his head to the side with his eyes closed. Adam sighed. "Okay then. So stubborn." He twisted one of Chad's nipples, and Chad's eyes flew open.

Adam chuckled and walked back to his ass and balls, perfectly presented for him and at just the right height. He'd had this bench built specially for this, not wanting to clutter his home with actual equipment like they had at the club. This bench had always suited his needs perfectly.

Slipping on a condom and lubing it well, he worked the plug in Chad's hole, angling it to rub against his prostate. Chad whimpered again as he pulled it out. Using the sharp knife he brought with him, he cut through the thin ropes holding Chad's legs and pushed his knees up to his chest, draping his calves over his arms. Adam took his dick in his hand and tapped it against Chad's hole.

"Can you feel me, baby? I'm going to fuck this little hole, and you still aren't allowed to come."

Chad groaned and with one smooth motion, Adam thrust inside, into the velvet heat of Chad's body. Fucking him deep and hard, he rocked against him. "Like this, boy?" At Chad's incoherent cry, he slowed way down, still thrusting deep, but taking it achingly slow, easing out to the very edge of his flange before slamming back in.

"Oh God, Adam, please. Please, please let me come. I hurt."

"You know what to do, boy. You know what to say."

"I-I'm yours, okay? I'm your b-baby."

"Tell me who's in charge."

"You are—you're in charge, Sir. Only you."

Adam smiled at him. "Good boy." He pulled the cock ring off and thrust hard and deep. "Come for me, baby. Come now."

Chad came hard, with a primal grunting groan of relief and bliss. He could only stiffen his legs and buck up as much as the ropes on his waist and chest allowed, until he emptied himself and sagged back down on the bench. Adam followed quickly, straining against him, and when he'd finished, he sagged down between Chad's legs.

He allowed himself only a minute, before he quickly cut the remainder of the ropes holding Chad to the bench and helped him sit up. Chad's head dropped to rest on Adam's shoulder, and he wrapped both arms around his waist. Adam held him and stroked his back for a few minutes until Chad caught his breath and calmed. Adam reached below the bench and retrieved a bottle of water, still cool from where he'd put it there a half hour before. He held it to Chad's lips.

"Drink, Chad." Chad gulped at the water, drinking almost half of it down before Adam stopped him. "Enough for now. I'm getting up to start the shower, baby, to clean us both off. Will you be okay for a few seconds?"

Chad nodded. Adam kissed his cheek and headed to the bathroom. He adjusted the water to be warm, but not too hot, and came back for Chad. He had to help him up off the bench and support him. The shower stall was huge in the master bath, so he walked in with Chad and angled his body under the warmth of the shower spray. Chad leaned his back against Adam's chest, and Adam reached for the soap. Taking some in his hands, he smoothed it over Chad's body, over his stomach and thighs. He lathered gently over his cock and balls, and turned him so he could get all the lube from his back side. When he had him clean, he turned off the spray, helped him from the shower stall and dried them both off with big fluffy towels.

Chad had begun to recover, but he still wanted to cling to Adam, and Adam let him, wrapping an arm around his waist as he supported him to the king-sized bed. He tucked Chad in and slid in behind him, spooning him and holding him close. Kissing the side of his face, he whispered soothing words in his ear and gently rubbed his hand over his chest. "Go to sleep, sweet boy. Things will be better in the morning."

Chad sighed and snuggled back into him. Within a few seconds, Adam heard his soft snores. Adam relaxed as well, exhausted now that it was over. He'd done it. He'd gotten his sexy, pseudo straight boy cop to not only have sex with him the night before, but to submit to him totally the very next night. He'd made him say he was his and only his and give up all his rigid control. Now only one question remained. Could he follow Cole's advice from earlier and give up some of his own rigid control? Could he compromise to keep a man he'd grown much too attached to in an effort to make it work? Christ, now that he had him, what in the hell was he going to do with him?

7

Chad woke up slowly, aware that an alarm was buzzing insistently nearby. He opened his eyes and found two warm brown ones staring back into his.

"Good morning, baby. Sleep well?"

Chad started to answer, but found his tongue was too fuzzy. It felt like it had grown hair since the day before. He nodded instead, rapidly blinking his eyes.

"I have a class, but I'm coming home early. Not much sleep last night for either of us, huh?"

Again, Chad nodded, feeling sluggish and almost drugged with sleep. What the fuck was he doing in Adam's bed? Memories of the night before came rushing back in, and he moaned.

"Go back to sleep," Adam told him, rolling over to sit up on the side of the bed. "It's still early. I'll reset the alarm for nine, okay?"

He didn't even remember responding. Closing his eyes, Chad tumbled back into a sound and untroubled sleep. It wasn't the alarm that woke him up the next time. It was a steady pounding at the door. Forcing his eyes open he rolled out of bed, dragging Adam's robe to him as he staggered, nearly stumbling down the hall to reach the front door.

"Rise and shine, Williams. Did I wake you? Well, too damn bad. I've been up all fucking night." Johansen brushed past him and stood in the foyer, looking around. "Professor already gone to work?"

"Yeah, I guess," Chad said, rubbing his face. "Sit down or something. Let me go splash some water and uh…"

"Yeah, yeah, whatever. Go ahead."

Walking down the hall to his room, Chad noticed how goddamned sore he was, and not just his asshole, which was plenty sore enough, but his damn dick and his balls too. He stood in front of the toilet to piss and a sudden picture of Adam standing by his open legs, slapping his balls and his prick with an open hand brought a hot flush to his face. He finished and hurried over to the sink to splash cool water on his face and neck again and again. After brushing his teeth and using a towel to dry off a little, he hurried back to his room to get dressed.

Thoughts of Phillips were teasing around his consciousness, and he was trying to hold them at bay, though they didn't seem so overwhelming this morning as the night before. Adam had taken some of that away from him. Wasn't that what he'd said? He no longer had to feel responsible or anxious over it, but the sadness was still there. Phillips had always been a good friend to him, maybe the best he had in the department, despite the difference in their ages.

He walked back to the living room and past where Johansen was slouching in the big easy chair and went straight to the refrigerator, looking for a cola. Predictably not finding any, he did locate some orange juice and poured himself a glass before he flopped down on the love seat where he'd been the night before. Another quick image of Adam holding him close with his hand down the front of his jock strap hit him, but he pushed it firmly away and concentrated on, Johansen who indeed, must not have slept a wink all night. He looked like hell.

"Can I get you anything?" he finally remembered to ask, but Johansen shook his head.

"I'm sloshing when I walk now, I've had so much coffee." He stared down at the floor between them for a moment. "Hell of a thing about Phillips, huh?"

"Yeah." Chad took a long drink of his juice and swallowed hard over the lump in his throat. "Any idea yet why he never called for backup?"

"No and that wasn't like him. Phillips did everything by the book, usually. "I'm thinking he just didn't get a chance to. They found burn marks on him from a stun gun. The guy must have slipped up behind him. He was shot with his own gun."

"Christ. What was he even doing there at that time of night?"

Johansen sighed. "We went for coffee after we left you. When your professor questioned us, it was pretty damn apparent we have nothing, and it bothered us both. Phillips liked to talk things through sometimes, try to get a handle on things, and something that guy Benjamin LeCroy said was nagging him."

"Like what?"

"LeCroy said he and his sub sometimes did public scenes at that club they all went to, and that they'd done one last weekend."

"Yeah, I remember they said something about it."

"Did you see it?"

Feeling uncomfortable at the way the conversation was going, Chad

94

drained his glass and put it on the coffee table, stalling for time. "No, we'd already left by that time."

"Oh. Well, Phillips remembered that one of the other couples had been to the club just before they were killed, and in checking his notes, he found they had also done a public scene. He was going to check into the other couple, but in the meantime, he wanted to know if the scene thing they did had any similarities."

"And did it?"

Johansen nodded and pulled out a small notepad from his pocket, looking down at it. "I asked him after... after they took Phillips...All three couples were using what they call CBT on their subs."

"Cock and ball torture. I've heard of it."

LeCroy said he used sounding rods on his partner. "Sounding?"

"Yeah, that's what Adam calls it."

"I figured it must hurt like a bitch. I had to have a catheter once and that hurt bad enough."

"What is it exactly? I never found out what it entailed."

"According to Adam, it's a set of surgical steel rods, going from really thin to about the thickness of your little finger. They put them down inside their subs' dicks, into the uretha."

Shaking his head, he went on. "One of the other couples did the same thing, which leads me to think the perp might have been in the club and witnessed it. Set him off in some way."

"We need to double check all the employees, the members, and all their guests."

"The guests are hard since they don't register in any way, but we will again, even though nothing turned up before. You're the only one who has gotten us any leads. He never baited us off before. The shrink says as well as escalating, he's challenging us to catch him, teasing us because he either knows or suspects we're watching his possible victims. The problem is we don't have the manpower to watch them all as much as they should be. Philips getting killed is proof of that. It's just like you said, someone should be watching the houses when they aren't home as well as following them. I think it may be up to you to set him off and bring him to where we can concentrate our efforts." He paused with a deep breath he let out slow. "Something else you need to know. Jeremy Rubin has disappeared."

While Chad stared at him in disbelief, he continued. "He left the house last night on foot, took off between a couple of houses, and they lost him."

"Before he killed Philips?"

"We don't know it was him. The gay killer has never used a gun before."

"You don't really believe it was a coincidence that Philips was killed at that house after being taken down with a stun gun?"

"No. Neither does anyone else." Johansen admitted. "The timing all fits.

Rubin left his house in more than enough time to get here, leave those notes, and get to LeCroy's to set things up. This time he did break in through a back window, another break in his MO, but seeing all of you at Morrison's he knew he had time and no one was home. The shrink says he's adjusting to circumstances. He hasn't returned to the preacher's house since, probably spooked over the shooting."

"What's his brother say?"

"They haven't questioned him. They're thinking there's a chance he might go back after he calms down and don't want to give our interest in him away. Your gig is about the only hope we have of drawing him out where we can control the situation."

Chad shook his head with a weak laugh. "You're suggesting I do a scene?"

"Right," Johansen said with a nod. "If you pretend to let the professor do a scene in that club this weekend that includes some of that CBT that might flip the killer's switch again."

"Fuck. You can't pretend something like that. You either do it or you don't."

Johansen smiled shortly. "Sounds like some medieval torture, doesn't it? There must be some way to fake it. No one expects you to actually do it, of course. Morrison could just make something look good and not really…"

"No," Chad interrupted. "The people at the club aren't stupid. Again, there isn't any way to fake it. I'd have to let him do it for real. At least once, anyway."

Squirmed uncomfortably in his chair, Johansen suggested, "Maybe there's something else you could do."

"I doubt it, not one that would work as well. No, it's a good idea. It could draw out the killer. Just—don't let it get out around the department, okay? Those assholes rag me enough as it is. Keep this quiet, just between us and the chief."

Johansen nodded. "You got it, but only if it won't harm you. The chief will never go for that."

"A good Dom never harms their sub. I've learned that much. No, nothing is forced in, from what I've read. These guys know what they're doing."

"Look, I know this must be really hard on you. I mean, being around all of this and having to pretend you're—well—not only gay, but kinky. You got more balls than I got, and I admire you for it. I don't think I could do it, let alone what I'm suggesting you do."

Chad nodded, self-conscious and uneasy. "So far it hasn't been so bad. Morrison is a decent guy."

"Good, good. You know, no one would blame you if you couldn't do any of this. I mean if you decide not to."

"Yeah, I know."

Johansen rose wearily to his feet. "So tomorrow is Tuesday. Think you can work something out by this weekend?"

"Yeah, maybe. I'll have to ask Morrison about it. He may not even agree. He said he isn't into giving pain."

"I thought about that. If not, maybe this LeCroy could do it, with Morrsion assisting, or whatever. You can ask him."

Chad barely suppressed a shudder at the idea of Benjamin LeCroy doing something like that to him, with or without Adam. "I'll talk to Morrison," he said. "I need to find out more about it before I agree to it completely."

"Oh yeah, sure." Johansen walked toward the door. "I...uh...I'll let you know when they make arrangements for Phillips."

"I'll go down to the station later and see if they need any help."

"No, the chief doesn't want you to take a chance on breaking your cover, not after knowing how close that bastard got to you last night, especially since you received those notes. That's why I came here. If anyone is noticing, it'll look like I'm just interviewing you."

"Okay, but damn it, I'd like to help out."

"What you're doing is helping more than any of the rest of us." He shook his head. "Poor Phillips. Hell of a thing. Only a few months from retirement." Still shaking his head while Chad walked him to the door, he turned to look back at Chad before he got in. "I'm going home to get some rest. Call me tonight and let me know what you decide."

Chad nodded and waved before closing the door and going back to the living room. He picked up his glass to rinse and put in the dishwasher, and then wandered back up to Adam's bedroom. Adam had cleaned everything up from the night before. All Chad had to do was make the bed. He slipped off his clothes and stretched out on it instead, staring up at the ceiling. He was exhausted, and his head hurt. He almost felt like he had a hangover, probably from all the adrenalin the night before. It was barely nine-thirty, and he had nowhere to go and little to do before Adam came home.

Adam—it seemed his whole life revolved around Adam now. How had that happened? He heard Adam's voice in his head. D/s relationships tend to get serious fast. Sharing that much intimacy with another person is different from any other relationship. Was that what he had now, an honest to God relationship with a Dom?

I am so fucked. This is not happening. He rolled over and pulled a pillow over his head.

* * * *

Adam got home around noon, after phoning the dean and telling him he had taken ill and needed to skip his last class. It was partially true. The news about the older detective who had questioned him so respectfully did make him sick to his stomach, not to mention, Chad's certainty that the killer had really been after Benjamin and Paul.

Benjamin could be a prick at times, but he was one of Adam's oldest friends, their common proclivities making them even closer than they might have been otherwise, and Paul seemed to be a decent enough person, though he didn't know him all that well. It wasn't a good idea to pay too much attention to another man's sub, after all, one reason for his irritation the night before when he saw the way Benjamin looked at Chad.

Despite his best intentions, he'd already started to think of Chad as his. He'd known it was unwise. Chad was still not out to anyone, even himself, let alone ready to admit his submissive nature freely. Adam had no idea what Chad would do when the case was over, but as Cole privately said to him the night before, if he really cared for Chad, he was going to have to make some compromises. Adam knew it was obvious to everyone that Chad wasn't totally comfortable with the submissive role he'd taken on. Cole's comment came after seeing Adam over the years with several subs and none, he said, had ever put that look in Adam's eyes. He'd winked and added that it was time for Adam to settle down with someone who really mattered to him. Adam was beginning to think he was right.

He enjoyed vanilla sex as much as the next guy, and if it was a deal breaker with Chad, then he could go along with that—for the rest of his life if he had to—even though kink was something that added spice, and he enjoyed it. He actually believed Chad enjoyed it, too, or at least some of it. He knew Chad would probably hate performing at the club and being on display. Adam could live without that, like Cole did. He would do that for Chad and still count himself lucky to have him. In the bedroom now—that might be a different story. Compromise? Wasn't that what Cole was talking about?

When he let himself in the front door, the house was quiet, even though Chad's car was parked in the driveway. Usually, he had the television going night and day, even if he wasn't watching it. Dropping his briefcase in the living room, he checked Chad's room. He wasn't there. Hearing soft snores coming from his bedroom, he went down the hall and stood in the door, gazing at Chad, sound asleep in his bed.

Lying on his stomach, the round, perfect globes of his ass were only partially covered by the sheet. He must have made some noise, because Chad rolled over on his back and saw Adam standing there. He smiled and stretched lazily. Adam slowly shed his clothes as Chad watched him, never moving, never saying a word. Naked, Adam walked to the side of the bed and looked down at him, all warm and sexy and totally delicious.

Before Chad could argue or agree, he climbed up on top of him and put his knee between his thighs, pushing them apart. When Chad lay back complacently and stared up at him smiling, he lowered his head to take his lips in a soft kiss. Chad's hands ghosting over his back in response. Adam pulled his head back to look at him and couldn't resist going in for more kisses on his lips, his throat, and his chest. He pressed his cock against Chad's, rubbing them together and eliciting a soft moan of pleasure.

Chad rubbed his thumbs against Adam's nipples, working them gently with his fingertips, then pushing Adam up, he angled his head up to lick them while Adam arched his back, giving him full access.

When he could speak again, he whispered into Chad's ear. "I missed you this morning. Did you miss me?"

Chad nodded breathlessly, seeming unable to form words while Adam's fingers massaged his balls. Adam stretched out to open the drawer in the bedside table for a condom and the lube. Up on his knees, he rolled on the condom and squeezed a generous amount of lube on his fingers and cock. Lifting Chad's leg onto his shoulder, he spread the lube over his tight, puckered hole. He kept one hand busy stroking Chad's cock. Slipping one fingertip up inside Chad, he teased in and out in a gentle motion.

Chad eyelashes fluttered, and Adam groaned, pushing in deep, adding another finger and working them in and out. Pressing up and slightly forward, he searched for the sweet spot and found it, watching the beautiful face in front of him come apart.

"Adam, please, harder, please."

Sliding his hand down the length of Chad's cock, his thumb slid over the slit and dipped inside, causing Chad to arch his back, cry out and come hard, spurting all over Adam's chest and his own stomach. Before he could finish, Adam's arm shot out, hooking under Chad's other leg, raising that delightful ass up and pulling Chad to him. He had to be inside him and thrust, deep and hard, unable to hold back, too aroused to be gentle. At the same time, he pumped Chad's cock through his orgasm, milking him dry.

Chad's fingers clawed into Adam's shoulders, holding on as he was ridden without mercy, Adam burying himself all the way in, his balls slapping against Chad's sweet ass. With a cry Adam came hard, arching up over him, his body convulsing until he collapsed, kissing Chad's face and his neck, licking and nipping at him in his passion. For at least three minutes, he trapped Chad beneath his weight, catching his breath and regaining his calm. The climax had been mind-blowing, excruciating, fucking wonderful, like it was every time with this man.

Pulling out, even though he didn't want to, he rolled to the side of the bed, squeezing Chad's hand before walking into the bathroom to clean up. Taking back a warm, wet cloth, he cleaned his lover tenderly. Chad allowed it, watching his every move with those amazing eyes. Adam fell back down beside him, tossed the cloth through the bathroom door to the tile floor and kissed Chad once more before leaning on his elbow and gazing down at him.

"This would be a perfect thing to come home to every day," he said, trailing a finger down Chad's abs and tangling in the soft hair of his groin.

"I could get used to it myself," Chad said with a little smile.

"Could you?" Adam asked, a little too sharply.

Chad laughed uneasily and sat up. "C'mon, professor. I've been in bed all day, it seems like. I need to talk to you about something."

Adam rolled back over on his back and sighed. Deflecting and changing the subject won't help you, boy. We're going to have this conversation, and soon.

* * * *

"No."

That was the answer Chad expected. He hadn't expected it to be quite so emphatic or with a touch of anger in Adam's voice. "I know you think I'm not ready."

"I know you aren't."

"Then get me ready. We've got four days before—"

"No. We will not discuss it any further."

"Yes, we will. This may be the only chance to aim him in the right direction and pick him off. Our resources are spread too thin."

"Exactly. Which is why he was able to leave those notes without any one seeing him. Though you may incite him to attack, there is no guarantee it's us he would attack or that the resources would be able to protect us. No."

"I would have—"

"I will not put your well-being in jeopardy."

"You think I can't take it? Is that the problem?"

"Oh, for God's sake, Chad. Petting you in front of four men made you uncomfortable. What do you think something like that in front of a room full would do to you?"

"I'll close my eyes," Chad offered.

Adam shoved up from his chair, stalking into the kitchen. Chad wasn't about to give up. He followed. "You'd be there protecting me."

"It will hurt, Chad. Nothing more than you can take, but it's uncomfortable. It's called torture for a reason."

"You'll take care of me."

"No." He opened the refrigerator, taking out salad makings. "I find your persistence in this kind of odd. Could it be you think you actually want to do this?"

"Maybe I do. You said that's what you'd do if I were your sub—explore my boundaries."

"You're not my sub. You're my—shit, I don't know what you are or

100

even what you want to be. I have feelings for you, though, and I'm tired of pretending I don't."

Chad walked up behind him and wrapped his arms around Adam's waist. "I have feelings for you too," he said, softly. "They scare the shit out of me, but I do have them."

Adam turned around in his arms and cupped his hands around Chad's jaws. "You don't have to say this, Chad. You're just reacting to what's happened between us. I was your first, after all."

"I know what I'm feeling."

Adam's eyes searched his face for a long moment before he sighed and rested his forehead against Chad's. "You have to take this slowly. You have to be sure this is what you want. I think for now we should keep our relationship very vanilla, no kink at all. Then later, if we both want to explore any of…this, we can."

Chad smiled. "Jeez, you like to have a plan, don't you? Part of that control freak thing? Let's just take it as it comes, Professor. One day at a time."

"We can do that, I guess," Adam said with a smile. "But no sounding."

"Oh we're back to that, huh? You giving the orders? Look, do you even know how to do it?"

"Of course I know. But I don't think—"

"Yeah, yeah, you don't think I'm ready. I get that, but from what I've been reading, it sounds kind of…well…intriguing. Look, can we try it at home at least? Just you and me, and then if I hate it and can't do it, we stop and forget about the club."

"Of course, we'd stop if you hated it and couldn't do it. You think I'd force you?" Adam sighed. "Okay. We'll try it. Go in the bedroom and lie on your back on the bed, while I get things ready."

Nervously, Chad walked down the hallway, wondering if he really should have pushed so hard for this. He thought about how it would be with Adam doing it, though, and immediately relaxed. Adam would never allow him to get hurt. Not any more than he wanted to, anyway. He had absolute trust in him.

* * * *

Lying on his back on Adam's bed, Chad skimmed his hand over his erection and waited for the sound of Adam's footsteps coming down the hall. Adam had already been in to find his box of sounding rods in his chest and left again, saying he needed to disinfect them thoroughly. When he heard him coming back, Chad got a momentary tight feeling in his chest, but it was gone as soon as Adam walked back in with an armload of things. Putting everything on the floor by the bench, he came over to Chad's side with the thinnest rod, which still looked insanely long and way too thick to have any chance of going inside him.

"This is it. Are you still sure?"

Chad took a deep breath, his eyes on the rod, but nodded.

Adam looked down at him and smiled. "This is not a scene. More like an experiment, okay? Still we need to have you tied down. I don't want you flinching or moving involuntarily and hurting yourself. So if anything hurts too much, or you want to stop, just tell me or use your safe word. Whichever comes to mind." He put the rod back in its case and ran his hand lovingly over Chad's cock. "This is very precious to me, you know."

He nodded toward the bench. "C'mon. Let's get you on the bench and tied down securely." Chad followed him to the bench and lay down on his back while Adam quickly fixed the ropes. He took his time, moving too slowly for Chad's nerves, but finally he was satisfied.

"Try to move, baby," Adam directed as he stood over him, watching carefully.

Adam was able to squirm a little, but couldn't really move.

"Is anything too tight?"

"No, it's good."

"Okay, let's get started. First of all, you can't be erect." He pressed his lips together, thinking hard. "Try thinking about unpleasant things first."

Chad smiled. "Like what?"

"I don't know, like coming out to your parents or to the people at work. Like picturing your mother's face as she watches you having sex, maybe…"

Chad's eyes widened, and he flinched at the idea. At the first mention of his parents, his erection, which had become rock hard as he was being tied, began to flag a little. He squeezed his eyes tightly shut and concentrated on his mother's face, then his father's and what they would think if they could see him and knew what he was about to do. It didn't take long for his excitement to wane.

Meanwhile, Adam moved around and by the time Chad reopened his eyes, he stood at the foot of the bench, between Chad's knees and his perfectly positioned genitals. He was putting a seriously thick coating of lube on the thin rod. He glanced over at Chad's progress and grunted in satisfaction. He came to Chad's side and used the lube left on his fingers and swiped them over Chad's slit, then rubbed the lube inside as deep as he could reach.

"Beginning now," he said, picking up Chad's limp penis and holding it upright in his hand. "It's going to hurt, Chad, but once it's inside, it'll feel very good. If you want to stop at any time, if it gets to be too much, just say so."

Despite or maybe because of his words, any remaining excitement Chad might have felt disappeared quickly. Trembling, he lifted up his head to watch, straining against his bonds. In an almost clinical manner, Adam poised the rod above his slit, pried back the small hole with one hand, while letting go with the other. Just like that, the well-lubed rod sank gently, slowly down into his penis. Using gravity alone, Adam allowed the thin rod's weight to push it down. At no time, did he add pressure or try to force it inside, yet after an initial feeling of discomfort and feeling of fullness, a dull, burning pain started up. It grew stronger, and Chad whimpered, then gasped. Even though he meant to stay still, tried to will himself not to move, he struggled for a moment or two against his bonds. He was very glad Adam had tied him down. Adam massaged his thighs and caught his gaze.

"Hurts," Chad whimpered with the rod almost halfway in.

Adam spoke quietly and soothingly. "We can stop any time you say. You don't have to do this."

Chad let his head fall back on the bench and shook his head. "No," he said, his voice low and guttural. "Don't stop."

Adam fingered Chad's hole, pressing a lubed fingertip inside, twisting it slowly as he watched Chad's face. Chad's focus switched to the finger in his ass, as his mouth fell open in surprise at the unexpected feeling of pleasure in the midst of the pain. Adam moved his finger slowly in and out, slipping a second finger inside, and Chad's eyes rolled back in his head.

"You're doing so well, baby boy. So well. Does it feel good?"

Chad opened his mouth to say no, when he realized it actually did feel good. In surprise, he raised his head again to check the progress of the rod and found it already inside, just a tiny bit sticking out of his slit, a little ball on top holding it in place. Adam still held his dick upright with one hand, while the other finger fucked him wickedly. He felt impossibly full and stuffed, but it wasn't unpleasant. Instead, it added to the pressure of Adam's fingers in his ass.

"You look beautiful, baby." Adam moved the tip of the sound. The feeling of pressure inside his cock was incredible. No longer exactly painful, the slight movement and resulting burn made him gasp.

"Going to fuck your slit now," Adam murmured, pulling the sound up the smallest bit before dropping it back. The words and the burn rocked Chad, but set up kind of yearning inside him at the same time. He moaned and thrashed his head, and Adam moved the sound again, coming higher this time before letting it fall back. At the same time he crooked his fingers and found Chad's prostate, giving it a rub as the sound fell back down. Chad almost came undone. Again and again Adam played with the sound and his gland, and Chad's whole world narrowed down to just the sensations in his cock and his ass.

"Please, please," Chad begged and with one swift, smooth move, Adam pulled the sound straight up and out, while pressing down hard on his prostate. Chad screamed and came so hard he almost passed out. Adam wrapped his hand around Chad's cock, so empty now, and milked him though his orgasm until he came to a shuddering stop, his breath coming in short gasps.

Chad was numbly aware of Adam untying the ropes, freeing him, and gathering him up in his arms to hold him tenderly.

"That was…that was…"

Adam held Chad to his chest, crooning to him and letting him recover. "Shh, catch your breath, babe. Don't try to talk yet."

"I-I love you, Adam. Love you."

"I know, sweet boy, I know." He pulled back and gazed down at Chad. "You're flying a little, huh? Just relax. I've got you."

Adam sat beside him, holding him for a long time before supporting him over to the bed and putting him down on his back. He lay down beside him, fully clothed. "Rest for a minute, baby, then tell me how you felt."

"I-I'm okay. Really. It burned, but felt incredible at the same time. Knowing that you were doing it to me…I could see your face and see it turning you on."

Adam smiled and shook his head. "Not at your pain, baby, but your excitement. I could see how it was making you feel, and I controlled that excitement. I was the one bringing that to you and bringing you pleasure. It's a heady feeling, I admit."

Chad turned toward him and buried his face against his neck, loving the warm feel of him.

Adam held him quietly for a few moments longer and then gently cleared his throat. "Uh…what you said at the end…you said…"

"I said I love you," Chad murmured against his throat. He raised his head and stared into Adam's eyes. "Never thought I'd say that to another man, but it's true. I love you, Adam."

Adam's eyes glowed softly as he stared down into Chad's. "This is just the after-glow talking, baby. You don't have to say this."

"You think I'm drunk off the feelings, huh? No, I'm not. I think I felt this way for a while now, but I couldn't say it, couldn't believe it was possible."

"Chad…"

"No, hear me out." Chad put his fingertips over Adam's lips. "I'm not trying to freak you out or anything. I don't expect you to say it back or return my feelings. Really. I just wanted to say it, wanted you to know."

Adam moved Chad's fingers gently aside and smiled at him. "But that's what I wanted to talk to you about. I-I have feelings for you too. I…um…shit, why is this so hard to say? I love you too. I didn't expect to, and it's thrown me for a loop." He searched Chad's face carefully. "I was thinking of asking you to move in with me, to see if you like it, to see if we can make it work."

Chad's mouth opened in surprise, and Adam rushed on. "Not like a sub or anything. I don't think you'd be comfortable that way. But if you think it's something you'd like to do—living here with me—then we could work out the details as we went along. I know this is fast, but..."

"Yeah," Chad said. "It is, but it feels right. I don't know. Can I think about it? I'm not even out to my family yet, and I need to take care of that as soon as I can. I still wouldn't be comfortable at work, yet. Could you live with that?"

Adam nodded. "You have to move at your own pace, sweetheart. Take it one step at a time. But what if you couldn't work it out with the people at the station? If it got to be too hard?"

Adam rubbed little circles on his back. Feeling safe and warm in the cradle of Adam's arms, Chad never wanted to move. "If they acted like the assholes they are, you mean? I don't know. There are other jobs, I guess. Other departments. What I do in my private life shouldn't matter."

"It shouldn't, babe, but in real life, it still happens. We live in the Bible Belt south, too, honey. You have to know that as cosmopolitan as the University can be, we're still in a small, southern town."

Chad laughed softly against his neck. "Are you trying to talk me into this or out of it?"

"Neither. I want you to know what you're getting into, though. Really understand that people can be so vicious. Like those boys in our group at church. How could a parent turn their back on their own child like that? Yet it happens all the time."

Chad nodded. "Not to mention this sick bastard doing the killings. I want to stop him so bad. See him pay for what he's done."

"I know, baby. Me too."

"So you'll agree to do the scene? In the club? It could be that he's a member there, and we can draw him off Benjamin and Paul."

"Chad, doing this here, with just the two of us, is still so totally different than doing it in the club, with everyone watching. I don't know if you're ready for that."

"If I'm not, then I can safeword, right? You said, no one would think anything bad about me doing that, right?"

"Of course not, but Chad, I don't want to scare you to death or traumatize you in any way."

"Look, I know this is moving way fast, and you'd never allow it otherwise. What's important is this could be a chance to draw the killer out, and I've proven I can do this, right?"

Adam chuckled. "Stop punctuating every sentence with right. You're not going to make me say it. No, I still don't like it." At Chad's exasperated sigh, he held up a hand. "But I will do this. We'll say we want to do a scene, and I'll have Benjamin helping." At Chad's horrified look, he smiled. "He won't touch you, I promise. I'll clue him in to what we're doing, and even if he can be a bit of an asshole, he's an experienced and very good Dom. Once we get started in the scene, you pretend to panic and you safeword."

Chad started to protest again, and Adam shook his head. "I insist. You use your safeword, and I'll pretend I'm reluctant to stop. Benjamin will insist and make a little scene about it. You act terrified, and that will get the dungeon masters involved if they're not already. It'll cause a commotion, and that's what we want." He smiled down at Chad. "Right?"

Chad grinned back at him. "Sounds good, but that would hurt your reputation, wouldn't it?"

Adam shrugged. "Maybe—I don't know. This is more important than my reputation, and eventually what we've been doing will all come out in the open. I don't think I'll be attending the club so much in the future anyway if you accept my invitation. What do you say?"

Chad leaned up and took his lips in a searing kiss that left them both breathless. "I say, you're on, Mister, but for now, I think one of us is wearing way too many clothes.

☐

8

"Nervous?" Adam asked, reaching over to squeeze Chad's hand. They were on the outskirts of Atlanta and would reach the club soon. Chad smiled back at him and shook his head.

"Not really. A little nervous about taking off my clothes for the scene, but that's about it."

Adam nodded. "I understand, but I'll be with you every second, baby. Keep your eyes focused on me and ignore everyone else."

"I'll try. Sir..." He smiled over at Adam and got a smile in return. Chad was jittery and determined to hide most of it from Adam.

In the past couple of days, Chad's nervousness had grown by leaps and bounds. He'd explained to Johansen what they planned to do, and he seemed greatly relieved and talked it over with the chief. Both agreed it could work, but cautioned Chad to only do this if he felt comfortable and trusted the professor to take care of him.

Johansen had been very frank with him. "Like I told you, you're a better man than I am to even think about this thing. If you think this professor might double cross you—like go ahead and do what he wants to once he has you...you know...tied down, then don't even think about this thing."

"I trust him with my life. He'd never do that to me or anyone else."

A long silence followed, and Chad swallowed hard. Maybe he'd said too much and was relieved when Johansen cleared his throat to ease the situation. "Okay, well good. Good that you feel that way. I'd still feel better if I was in the audience. How would you feel about that?"

Chad shifted nervously. "I-I guess so. Just...don't look at me, you know?"

"Well, hell, Chad, I have to look at you to make sure everything is okay. But...I understand what you're saying. I'll keep my focus on the professor. Believe me."

Chad laughed nervously. "Okay, then. I'll talk to Adam about getting you in. Our plan now is to be there around seven o'clock. Before it gets really crowded and wound up. Wear something that doesn't scream cop, okay?"

"Like what?"

"I don't know…do you have any leather pants? Or some tight jeans?"

"Well, hell no."

Chad laughed. "Buy some. Maybe take off your shirt. I don't know."

"Oh, no, not going to happen. I'll see what I can do, but don't expect much. I'm not looking to go home with anybody."

"Are you sure?" Chad teased. "I can totally see you as a bear. Want me to see if Adam can find you a date?"

"Oh very funny. Let me know how to get in and I'll be there."

"Okay," Chad said, laughing as he hung up.

That had been a couple of days ago, and he wasn't laughing anymore, dreading the idea of Johansen looking at his ass. He wouldn't though, would he?

Chad groaned, and Adam glanced over at him. "Second thoughts? We can call this off."

"No, I'm good. Just thinking about Johansen being there and seeing me naked."

"You won't take anything off until we start the scene. Once we begin, I'll be role playing. Treating you like my sub. Do you trust me, baby?"

"You know I do," Chad said warmly and put a hand on Adam's thigh.

"Good. I'd never harm you. Remember that. No matter what else happens."

"I know."

They reached the club, and Chad scanned the parking lot. Johansen's car was parked near the entrance, but it was empty. He'd apparently already gone inside as a guest, using Adam's name, the way they'd arranged.

Chad got out of the car, leaving his jacket inside as Adam locked the door. He was wearing the soft, satiny shirt Adam bought for him, buttoned over tight jeans that rubbed him a little. He wasn't wearing any underwear, figuring it would be less trouble when it came time to disrobe.

They went inside, and Chad was hit with the blast of music and smoke that filled the room. As a private club, they allowed smoking, and the smell of it made Chad's stomach roll a little. Adam dropped his hand from Chad's back and strode toward his usual table, already occupied by Benjamin and Paul, along with another couple Chad didn't recognize. He walked carefully at Adam's heel, remembering to keep his gaze down, even though he felt the heat of an occasional appraising glance at him as he passed. When they reached the table, Adam sat down, tossing a cushion from the chair down on the floor beside him. Chad sank down gratefully and leaned against Adam's leg, glad to be below eye level for a little while.

Adam had already spoken to Benjamin about the scene, explaining to him what they were doing, though Benjamin had no idea Chad was a cop. He knew his role in the scene, though, and agreed to do whatever he could to entice the killer and bring him to justice. The department had increased his surveillance for a couple of days as well, just in case. They couldn't be sure the killer hadn't decided, after Phillips' death, that the element of surprise was gone. The profilers thought he would move on to someone else—hopefully, Adam and Chad.

Adam's leg almost vibrated with tension, and Chad laid his cheek against it, trying to soothe him. Immediately, his fingers dropped down into Chad's hair, threading through it lovingly. "Okay, baby?" he asked quietly, and Chad nodded, giving him a little smile.

Benjamin, sitting across from Adam, caught his eye. He seemed different tonight, more serious and solemn. "Give me the word when you're ready, man," he said, and Adam nodded.

Chad glanced up and looked directly at him, though he knew he wasn't supposed to, and saw him give him the briefest of nods. Adam explained that Benjamin, though a little brash, was an experienced Dom and would never let a scene continue once a sub used his safeword, even if they hadn't already planned this out carefully.

"Ready as I'll ever be, I guess," Adam said. He tugged gently on Chad's hair. "Showtime, baby."

Adam and Benjamin got up, with Chad following behind Adam. Already another scene was in play nearby, involving three men and a flogger. A small group had gathered to watch. Not looking up, Chad followed Adam to a broad, padded bench, and at Adam's nod, he stripped off his clothes, folding them as he went and leaving them in a small pile on the floor. When he was naked, he glanced up and saw a few people had drifted over to watch, and a slight moment of panic hit.

Adam's hand touched his shoulder. "Look at me, boy. I'm the most important person in the room as far as you're concerned."

"Yes, Sir," Chad answered quickly, dropping his gaze back to the floor and standing in the presentation position, his hands behind his back. Adam walked around him, checking his posture, touching him occasionally to correct some minor flaw.

"Good," he said. "Good boy. Now get on the table on your back." Chad turned and hoisted himself onto the table. Benjamin and Chad secured him with the cuffs and straps attached to the bench. With both of them working quickly and expertly, they had him strapped down firmly in no time. Benjamin brought out the rods and the disinfectant and went to work cleaning the smallest rod, while Adam positioned himself on the far side of the bench at Chad's hips.

Adam picked up Chad's limp dick from his thigh. "Scared boy?" he said, chuckling. "You should be. I'm going to fuck your little holes until you beg for mercy. Gonna stuff this little boy cock and fuck you till you scream."

Chad swallowed hard, reassuring himself it was all role play and Adam wouldn't harm him. Even still, his heart raced out of control. He glanced over at the group of people who'd come to watch and saw no one he knew, but one man at the back of the crowd was wearing a leather hood. As Chad watched, the man, one of the dungeon masters, edged closer and closer.

Benjamin had finished cleaning the rod to his satisfaction and lubed it, spreading on a thick coat. Time to put on a show.

Chad groaned loudly. "Nooo, please. I don't want this. Please..."

Adam glared at him. "What's your safeword, boy?"

"Red to stop and yellow to slow down, Sir."

"Then use them if you're going to. Otherwise, take what I'm going to give you."

"Y-yes, Sir," he said softly.

Adam lubed his fingers and spread some over Chad's limp dick. He hadn't had to think about anything unpleasant to go soft. He was no exhibitionist, and the people standing close by watching had totally taken care of his erection.

Adam fingered him, and he focused on the ceiling. He wondered briefly if Johansen was in the crowd watching and decided he didn't want to know. Adam's fingers caused him to grow thicker, and a sharp slap to his balls, caused him to gasp with pain.

"Settle down, dirty boy, so we can get this first one in. Such a little slut. You love it, don't you?"

Chad whimpered and tried to close his legs when the slap came again. His eyes wide, craning his neck to look down at Adam. His steady brown eyes were gazing back at him, and he calmed down. Then he saw Benjamin step over and hold the rod over him. Adam took his penis in his hand and held it up as Benjamin lowered it slowly toward his cock.

"No!" Chad yelled. "No, red-red-red-red-red!"

Benjamin stopped immediately, but Adam snatched the rod from his hand, lowering it toward Chad's slit again.

"Nooo," Chad cried. "Red! Red!"

Benjamin grabbed Adam's wrist. "What are you doing? He used his safeword."

"He's a silly slut. He wants this. He's just scared."

"Exactly," Benjamin said firmly. "That's why we're done."

They wrestled for a moment over the rod, with gasps coming from the crowd. In what seemed like seconds, two dungeon masters were there, one taking Chad out of the straps while another spoke quietly and sternly to Adam, taking hold of his arm and leading him away.

Benjamin came to Chad's side and gave him his clothes, standing in front of him while he quickly pulled them on. People were pressing in on him from all sides, it seemed, and he looked around frantically to see where they were taking Adam, pulling back when Benjamin tried to take him back to the table.

Benjamin spoke softly in his ear. "It's okay. They won't hurt him, just settle him down and make him leave. We'll give it a few minutes and then go outside. He's going to be waiting for us."

Chad nodded and allowed himself to be steered back to the table, where Paul made a big fuss over giving him water and rubbing his back. Chad looked toward the entrance in time to see Johansen's broad back at the door, going outside. Good. He didn't like the idea of Adam being left on his own in the parking lot with the possibility of a killer present.

In a few minutes, Benjamin and Paul led him out of the club, walking on either side of him. As soon as they made it outside, Chad looked for Adam and found him standing by the car. He broke away from Benjamin and Paul and hurried over to him.

"Are you okay?"

Adam smiled down at him. "I'm fine. They suggested I don't come back for a while, but other than that, I'm good." Adam took hold of Chad's shoulders and gazed into his eyes. "What about you? Are you okay? I know you hated being undressed in front of everyone like that."

"I'm fine." He hugged Adam again, throwing his arms around his waist and putting his head on his chest.

Adam said their goodbyes to Benjamin and Paul, thanking them for their help, and got Chad into the car to go home. "If the killer wasn't actually in attendance tonight, and let's face it, the odds are probably against it, then we'll have to wait for word to get around. With Benjamin and Paul, there was no reaction for four days. Did the chief give you any indication about how much time went by after the other couple did their scene and the time they were killed?"

"No, but I'll check into it right away. We might be able to see some pattern. If the killer wasn't there, how would he have known about it?"

Adam shrugged. "Hard to say. Word does get around, though. The BDSM community is not all that large here in the area, and a lot of people know each other both in and out of the club."

"Well, we've done what we could to draw him out. Johansen didn't say it, but I know the chief must be getting pressured by the FBI to turn this case over to them, especially after what happened to Phillips. I wouldn't be surprised if this isn't our last chance."

"What will happen then? Will you be…moving out?"

"Leave you there on your own? Not a chance."

"Oh? The FBI wouldn't give me surveillance?"

"They would, but it's not the same as me being there. Assuming you still want me there?"

Adam smiled over at him. "What do you think?

"Oh, I don't know. You might get some sexy little FBI dude to move in. I still have one of those jocks I haven't used yet."

"I don't know if anyone else would look as good as you in them, but I mustn't be too quick to judge. I'd be willing to give him a chance."

"Yeah, over my damn dead body. And yours. I carry a gun, remember."

They both laughed and talked the rest of the way home, with Chad feeling like a weight had been lifted off his chest. The scene he'd been dreading was over and behind him, and he knew he'd done all he could to bring the killer out in the open. It was time to wait and see what happened, and if the FBI did take over the case, at least Chad knew he would be staying with Adam.

Things were bound to get out now to the entire department, but he found that he didn't care so much. There would be those who didn't accept him. If they didn't, so be it. Their loss. He was tired of living a lie to avoid upsetting or offending other people, who couldn't care less about his happiness.

Decision made, he felt lighter, freer than he had in years. Before he knew it they were arriving in Athens and on their way back to Adam's house. It was still fairly early, not even nine o'clock. All Chad wanted to do was relax and maybe watch a little television, but as they pulled into the driveway, a dark sedan pulled in behind them.

"Oh hell. This isn't something I appreciate tonight." Adam put the car in gear and glanced in his rear view mirror. "Preacher Rubin. Maybe I'll take out my checkbook now and head him off before he gets inside."

"No, invite him in," Chad said. "Maybe I can get some information out of him about where his brother may be, if there's any connection between him and the club Johansen hasn't been able to trace down. I'd also like to know how much bullshit he feeds everyone and how much is true. His lies are only making it harder to get a handle on Jeremy."

"Okay, but get rid of him as quickly as you can. I'm not in the mood for him tonight."

They got out of the car and waved to the minister as he approached, briefcase in hand.

"I'm so sorry to come by so late," he said. "But I was visiting some of my flock who also live on the cul-de-sac—the Robinson's. Lovely couple, do you know them?"

At Adam's abrupt nod, he continued, not catching the hint. "I saw your car pull in and thought perhaps I could kill two birds with one stone, so to speak. I'm collecting again for the shelter. We had a new emergency come in to the church last night, and I so want to be able to offer a better place as soon as possible."

"No problem, Reverend," Chad said. "Come inside, and we'll write you a check."

"So nice of you." Jason returned Chad's nod of greeting, but his eyes didn't make contact. He followed them to the door and stepped inside behind them.

"Make yourself comfortable while I get my checkbook," Adam told them and walked away.

"Thank you. This will mean so much to the boys who have no place to go."

The man seemed sincere enough, but he irritated Chad as much as the other men. "How are your plans going for the group home?" he asked. "Do you break ground soon?"

"I've been looking at property, but have found some resistance among potential neighbors. There is so much bias with so little understanding."

"Seems to me that with your family history, you'd have some prejudices yourself, like your brother does, from what I hear."

The minister shot Chad a strange look. "My brother's problems started when he walked in on our parents doing…well, doing something that shocked him. He screamed hysterically, thinking our father was hurting our mother. He was screaming, our mother was screaming that it was okay, that it was just a game they were playing, and my father couldn't get either one of them to shut up. He made my brother and I both go to the basement until he could um…extricate our mother from the scene they were playing and she could calm Jeremy down. It was quite traumatic and affected our father to a degree that he left the next day. We didn't see or hear from him for years. When we did, he was living with a man. He explained to us that Billy was his lover. As young as we were, it was difficult for us to understand."

Amazed at how much information the man handed out on such a private matter, and still wondering if any of it was true, Chad rocked on his heels. "Um yes, that must have been really upsetting for you. How old were you?"

"I was fourteen by then. Jeremy was sixteen. He blamed Dad's life style for him deserting us and for our parents' divorce."

"Was there ever a time when Jeremy, ah, like went to visit your dad and something happened to…" He waved his hand slightly. "…maybe intensify his anger or hatred?"

Jason gave a faint smile and shook his head. "Jeremy refused to ever visit him after that one time. He had a better understanding of what, or I should say, how two men could be lovers. It was a few years before I fully comprehended not only what a homosexual relationship entailed but understood our father was a Dom in a BDSM relationship."

"So then you understood why Jeremy hated him so much," Chad murmured in distraction. Was there even a kernel of truth in what this guy said?

"No, I found my peace in serving the Lord. I have never given up hope that someday Jeremy will find a way to release his anger, though with our father dead now there's no chance of a reconciliation. He may never have closure to the source of his inner rage."

That was the opening he needed. "And you said that was a couple of years ago?"

"No, only recently, a couple of months now."

The bastard was still lying. Chad still dug. "How did your mother take it all?"

"You mean when their marriage broke up? Devastated, of course. She suddenly found herself alone with two young boys. She'd never worked outside the home before then. It was very difficult for her."

"But she was into the lifestyle? The BDSM stuff?"

"Oh, no, not at all. She just loved him so much she went along to keep him from leaving her."

Chad jumped when Adam spoke up. He hadn't even been aware of him coming back into the room. "That doesn't seem very likely, Reverend. She may have told you that, but in a true BDSM relationship, the dominant partner only does what the more submissive partner is willing to do."

Jason gave him his weak smile. "I don't believe my father had any training then, though I believe he did afterwards."

Chad hoped Adam didn't take him off subject. As long as Jason was talking so freely, he wanted to get all the information he could, but his cell phone rang just then, before he could continue with his questions. He was prepared to ignore it until he saw Johansen's number on the ID. "Excuse me. I've got to take this," he told Adam.

"Of course."

Chad walked quickly down the hallway to the guest room and ducked inside. "Yeah?" he asked, closing the door to his room. "What have you got?"

"He was fucking adopted by his mother's second husband."

"Who's adopted? What the hell are you talking about?"

"The preacher. The mother finally returned my call. She verified the divorce, all right and then dropped a bomb. Rubin is her second husband's name. He adopted Jason. That's why we had trouble locating records on Jeremy. We were searching under the wrong fucking name."

"He didn't adopt both of them?"

"There is no Jeremy. Apparently the crazy bastard has a split personality. That's what I'm trying to tell you. Jeremy died when he was twelve years old. It's been the preacher all along."

Chad dropped the phone, jerked the drawer out of the nightstand to get his gun, and tore out of the room. He caught himself before he rounded the corner, took one deep breath to prepare himself, and charged into the room.

Everything was quiet except for some ragged breathing coming from the kitchen. He rushed toward the noise and was horrified to see Adam tied and gagged on the floor, unconscious, a dark pool of blood seeping out from under his head. Before he could get to him, a slight noise made Chad pivot around to see the preacher coming at him. Chad spun, his left arm catching the hand holding a stun gun aimed at him. Jason Rubin caught Chad's right wrist at the same time, keeping Chad from swinging his gun around for a shot at him.

Instinct and training kicked in along with a double surge of adrenalin. Chad stepped into him, aiming his right knee at Jason's crotch. The son of a bitch was fast and strong. He turned to take the blow to his hip, released the stun gun and twisted his wrist, loosening Chad's hold on him. One hand free, teeth bared, and growling, Jason lunged, going for Chad's throat. Chad swung his arm up, defecting Jason's arm, and reversed the action, back fisting Jason in the side of his head. Jason staggered back, but transferred his free hand, twisting Chad's thumb back from the grip of his gun. The gun clattered to the floor, and Chad didn't care. At a primeval level he wanted to kill. One hand squeezing Jason's throat, he didn't feel the punches Jason delivered. He delivered his own, holding Jason with one hand and pounding the face in front of him with the other. A vicious punch to the jaw, another punch to the face, another and another, he drove Jason to the floor. Knee in Jason's chest, Chad drew back for still another blow to the unconscious man's head when a strong arm grabbed him and pulled him sideways.

"That's enough!"

Not for Chad. He lunged forward only to have another arm snag him at the waist, spinning and pulling him away. A detective Chad only vaguely recognized stood in front of him, arms out to block him, while another knelt down beside Adam, speaking urgently on his radio.

"Enough," the man in front of Chad said. "He's down. Back off and calm down."

Adrenalin still coursed through his system, but Chad shifted his gaze toward Adam. Without a single thought of how it would look, or what the two men might think, Chad rushed to Adam and dropped to his knees beside him. He'd have jerked him up in his arms if the other man hadn't stopped him.

"Don't move him. The paramedics are on the way."

Calmed down marginally, Chad clenched his fists. He knew what the man was saying was right, but every instinct he had shouted at him to hold

Adam in his arms. He fought for control of himself and laid a hand on Adam's chest to at least satisfy himself Adam was still breathing. He swallowed hard in relief at the up and down motion beneath his palm. Brushing Adam's hair from his forehead, he leaned down and tried to look under him, searching for the source of blood still seeping onto the floor.

"Must have hit his head on the island when he fell," the man said, pointing to a spot of blood on the counter edge.

The man's name was Carlson, Chad remembered. He and the other man were one shift of the surveillance team. He nodded, not trusting himself to speak.

"At least now we know why there had been no forced entry. Once he knocked them down and tied them up, all he had to do was leave a door open, establish that he left, and sneak back after dark."

Chad nodded again, forcing himself up to his feet to pull open a drawer. He had a knife in his hand to cut Adam's bonds before Carlson stopped him. "Let the medics do that. You don't know that he didn't break an arm or something."

Christ, he couldn't do anything but nod like one of those crazy dolls, barely aware of what was going on around him for staring at Adam.

Carlson asked the other man, "How's he?"

"In worse shape than the guy in there. He beat the hell out of him."

"I meant to kill him," Chad murmured, finally finding his voice and from Carlson's reaction at the wrong time.

"Jesus, don't say that where someone else can hear you." He gripped Chad by the shoulder. "I know it's the adrenalin talking, but saying something like that could get you in a lot of trouble. It's a damn good thing Johansen called to get us in here before you did kill him. We never thought a damned thing about the preacher visiting."

Chad sat back down on his heels next to Adam, hand on his chest. "Where the hell are the medics?"

"They're here."

Sirens blared, the sound growing closer and stopping in the front yard. Johansen rushed through the door behind the paramedics, his head whipping around to take in the scene. He went straight to Chad and turned his head by the chin. "You okay?"

Bruises were beginning to sting and throb on his face, but he pulled away and nodded. His eyes never left Adam as the paramedics worked on him. Chad murmured, "I fucked up. The fucking preacher was right there in front of us the whole time, the connection to all of them. He knew them all, begging all the time for donations. I heard them talking about it and didn't put it together."

"Yeah, we all screwed up." Johansen looked nearly as sick as Chad felt. "I called the manager at the club on the way for confirmation. He worked there as a dungeon master, part-time under Jeremy's name, the last name of their natural father, not Jason's adopted father's. That's why it didn't raise a flag when we ran all the employees, and the hood kept everyone from recognizing him. Like I said, there is no brother, at least not anymore."

"How the hell did he fool everyone into thinking his brother was still alive?"

"From what we can tell, he's been living as both of them, switching back and forth, since his teen years, using Jeremy's birth certificate and social security number to create his alternate personality." He grimaced. "Things I was about to tell you when you hung up." He paused with another grimace. "His mother is on her way here to fill in some holes, but she was pretty upset with me to start with in questioning me about her dead son."

"Was any of that true about his father?"

"His real father, yes, not the man who adopted him."

"That's why he killed those men?"

"Really hard to say this early. The shrink thinks even though he hated his father and blamed the lifestyle for being deserted as a child, he was drawn to it, but never had the nerve to come out and live it openly. Maybe he hated gays for having the courage he lacked, or like we thought before, in some twisted way, they served as some kind of surrogates for punishing his father. The truth is, we may never know, unless he confesses, and as psycho as he is, we probably won't understand it even then."

Chad looked down, distraught as the paramedics carried Adam by him on a stretcher.

Johansen's hand slid out to grip and squeeze Chad's arm. "He'll be okay, just a bad bump on the head."

Chad shuddered, and his breath caught in a sob.

"Hold it together," Johansen whispered in his ear, "Unless you want the others to know."

Looking around, Chad could see the sidelong looks he was getting. "Fuck them. I'm in love with him."

"I know, or at least I thought that was what was going on with you. Philips could see it, too. Just keep it together and I'll take you to the hospital. You need to be looked at anyway."

Chad nodded, following the stretcher that moved past him, not that he thought he needed a doctor himself. At that moment, he didn't care about anything but Adam.

* * * *

"He's fucking crazy."

Chad stood in Johansen's office the next day, talking with him about the case. He hadn't left the hospital the night before until he knew Adam was out of danger no matter how insistent the chief had gotten. Though he was sore, his own injuries were minor. Once at the precinct, the day had been exhausting after the mother and everyone else involved had been interviewed extensively, he'd answered question after question and made out his written report. The whole time Jason/Jeremy shifted back and forth in a complete mental break, arguing with himself and refusing to answer questions.

"You're right. Without a doubt he's crazy. That story he told you about walking in on his parents was true except for the fact it was Jason who walked in, started screaming, and set everything else into motion. The shrink is theorizing that he twisted everything around, making Jeremy take the blame for everything he did wrong, possibly out of guilt. The mother has admitted that Jeremy was shouting at Jason to shut up after their father closed the basement door on them. That was when Jeremy died, by the way. She suspected an argument between them resulted in Jeremy falling to his death down the stairs. The shrink says that most probably is the incident that caused the personality split. The constant moving around after he left home was to keep people from realizing he was two people or an effort to run away from Jeremy."

Johansen sank into a chair, shaking his head. "I don't know if I've got this all straight, but the gist of it is Jason recognized he was gay, saw the damage his father's denial of his own sexuality caused to his family and genuinely wanted to help others. His alter personality, Jeremy, however, was projecting his hatred for his father and his own self-hatred onto other gay men, particularly Doms. He got a job as a part-time bouncer at the club so he could be around the men. The preacher personality gained entry to the homes of the victims, and then the Jeremy personality took over, punishing them, probably seeing them as surrogates in some way as his father and the lover that took him away from them."

"Most of that you told me already," Chad told him, his exhaustion sounding in his voice.

"I told you what the profiler thought, not what we know now. Did I tell you everyone thinks you were right about his real father's death being the trigger that set him off to kill?"

Chad nodded, not even wanting to hear anymore. "I need to get back to the hospital."

Johansen drew a deep breath before saying, "Some of the guys are making comments about you maybe liking your undercover gig more than you let on. If you don't want to feed the gossip mill any more, I suggest you stay away."

"I could care less what they think. Please tell the chief I need to get to the hospital. If he needs me, that's where I'll be."

"He's heard the rumors. Can't say what he thinks about it. I know he can't fire you over it."

Chad sighed. "If he wants to fire me because I'm gay, I suppose he can find a way. Adam and I did everything in our power to find the killer, to draw him out, and succeeded, even putting Adam's life on the line. If the chief wants to fire me after all we've done, there's not much I can do about it."

"Hey, hold on. I never said he wanted to do anything like that. Hell, he'll probably give you a promotion. I just didn't know if you wanted it kept quiet."

"No, I'm done hiding who I am. You see what it got Jason Rubin. Man, I don't know. He was probably crazy anyway, but all this shit over hiding who he really was never did him any good. That's for sure. At least five men are dead as a result." Chad shook his head. "I'm done with it. Let them have their fun and discuss me all they want. If you don't mind, just tell them it was me, the fag, the one who likes his kinky undercover gig, who stopped the damn killer. A cop killer, I might add. What the fuck did they do?"

EPILOGUE

Chad finished washing the car and went inside to find Adam with his lap full of papers, sound asleep. Moving quietly, he pulled the papers out of his lap and put them on the coffee table before plopping down in his lap and throwing his arms around his neck.

"What the hell?" Adam cried out. He hugged Chad and frowned playfully at him. "Trying to sneak up on me?"

"It wouldn't be hard, with you sound asleep."

Adam smacked the back of Chad's jeans clad ass and followed by a rub over it to soothe the sting. "I'm still recuperating. The doctors said to take it easy for a while, you know. I did have a concussion, after all."

Chad kissed his forehead. "That was over a month ago." Kissing him again, he added "Poor baby."

"You're going to think poor baby when I get through with you."

Adam wrapped a strong arm around him, locked him in place, and tickled him unmercifully. Chad rolled to the floor, and Adam followed him down, pinning his hands over his head and kissing him breathless.

"Mmm, maybe we should take this to the bedroom," Chad said against Adam's lips.

"Not a chance." Adam put his hand over Chad's groin, cupping him and the cock cage he wore. "This doesn't come off until tonight."

"Oh, come on, I even washed your car for you."

"Sucking up does not get you out of the cage until your time's up. I caught you beating off in the shower last night, and you know you're not supposed to touch yourself. That belongs to me."

Chad huffed out a breath. "You were already asleep when I got home, and I didn't want to wake you." He kissed Adam's neck. "Please, Sir."

"Now you call me Sir because you want to negotiate a scene. Nope. You know the rules." He dropped a final kiss on his lips before getting to his

120

feet and pulling Chad up beside him. He put his hands on Chad's ass and pulled him close. "Besides, when I let you come, it'll be totally worth it. Now sit down over there and behave. Tell me why you worked so late last night."

Falling back down on the sofa, Chad put his feet up on the coffee table, got a stern look and pulled them back on the floor. "Johansen was tying up the loose ends on the Jason Rubin case, and he let me hang around to read the final report."

"You and Johansen get along better now than you did before all this, don't you?"

"Yeah, he's been really cool. Stood up to some of the jerks in the department for me, and things have been a lot better, especially since the chief promoted me to sergeant." Chad grinned. "Of course, it helps that I can write them up if they get out of line, but everyone has been pretty cool about me moving in here with you. Besides, now that I know my parents are okay with having a gay son, I don't really care about anybody else. In fact, I think my mom likes you better than she likes me."

"Entirely possible. I'm taller and much more charming."

Chad laughed and threw a pillow at him.

He dodged it and smiled back at him. "So—anything new on the report?"

"Not really. They're satisfied he didn't start killing until his father died, leaving any unsolved cases out there, and the court appointed shrink says Jason-slash-Jeremy isn't competent for trial. No surprise."

"Well, at least the group home he was planning was real. He had all the money in a special account. Some of the deacons of the church are administering the funds and looking for a new preacher. I don't know if the congregation can survive the scandal of what he did, but I wish them luck."

"Me too." Chad was quiet for a few minutes, staring at the ceiling as Adam went back to work on grading papers. After a few minutes, Chad got up and stretched. "Well, I think I'll go lie down for a little while and take a nap. Late night last night," he said with a little smile.

"Yes, especially after I caught you. Have a nice nap," Adam said, distracted by the paper he was reading.

"It's only that I really was bad last night. I wouldn't have blamed you if you'd tied me to the bed and…ah…spanked me or something, you know, me being so stubborn and hardheaded and all. I really do need to learn my lesson…"

Adam put the papers down, the corners of his mouth turning up. "Oh really? You think you might need a spanking, Chad?"

"Well, I don't need it. I'm just saying I might deserve it, but you go ahead and grade your papers, Professor."

Adam stood up, took him by the hand, and pulled him toward the bedroom. "Oh, no. I think I have somebody that needs to be taken care of. I think I need to see to you right now.

Shannon West: www.shannonwestbook.com
Shannon West is an author of M/M romance. She publishes with Secret Cravings Publishing, MLR Press, Ellora's Cave and Siren Publishing, as well as publishing some independent books. Originally from Virginia, she now lives in Georgia with her very understanding husband and large family. A lover of M/M romances, she reads everything M/M she can get her hands on—purely for research purposes, of course. She loves men and everything about them, and believes that love is love, no matter the gender. A huge proponent of gay rights, she is a PFLAG mom. She supports equal rights for everyone. Though there are never enough hours in the day, she tries to work every day, giving in to the demanding men in her head and writing their stories. She's easy like that. Other than men, she loves traveling, reading and watching scary movies and ghost hunter shows on TV.

LL Brooks
LL is an author of both M/M and M/F erotic romance. She publishes with Secret Cravings Publishing, as well as independently. She lives with her husband in Arizona. She loves her family, traveling, and meeting her readers. Most days you can find her at her computer,

Made in the USA
Lexington, KY
25 January 2014